At that moment, the truth hit me.

Mead is an all-girl school. The last time I'd gone to school with boys was in third grade!

"I'm sure you'll make lots of new friends at Midway—boys as well as girls," Dad said.

"I don't want new friends," I wailed. "I'm happy with my old ones."

Dad reached for my hand. "Honey, the sooner you accept it, the better. If you can manage to look at the bright side—"

He babbled on and on, trying to make me feel better. I listened as long as I could, then I pulled my hand away and screamed, "Forget it! I'm not going! And you can't make me!"

NINTH GRADE OUTCAST

Avery Hart and
Paul Mantell

Cover by Bruce Emmett

Troll Associates

Library of Congress Cataloging-in-Publication Data

Hart, Avery.
    Ninth grade outcast / by Avery Hart & Paul Mantell.
      p.   cm.—(Midway Junior High)
    Summary: Megan's life takes a sharp turn when her father's new job
forces her to transfer from private school to the public junior high
school halfway through ninth grade.
    ISBN 0-8167-2392-3 (lib. bdg.)   ISBN 0-8167-2393-1 (pbk.)
    [1. Schools—Fiction.] I. Mantell, Paul. II. Title.
III. Series.
PZ7.H256274Ni 1992
[Fic]—dc20   91-2492

A TROLL BOOK, published by Troll Associates

Printed in the United States of America.

10 9 8 7 6 5 4 3 2

NINTH GRADE
OUTCAST

To anyone who ever felt left out.

CHAPTER

1

$\mathcal{S}$ometimes, life is absolutely perfect. Then, the next thing you know, it's the absolute pits. You might think I'm exaggerating, but I'm not. It actually happened to me.

The day before Christmas vacation started was a half-day of school. It also was the coldest day of the year. But since I still had Christmas shopping to do, I headed for downtown Meadsville with my best friend, Amanda Harding.

We probably looked pretty funny running down the street—a couple of ninth graders, all bundled up in our overcoats. At least the coats hid our ugly Mead Academy uniforms.

Amanda had her big red beret pulled way

down over her forehead. It completely covered her sleek brown bangs and swallowed up her blue eyes.

"How can you see with that thing on?" I asked her.

"X-ray vision," she said through chattering teeth. "Just three more blocks and we'll be at the bookstore."

"Three blocks? Ugh, it's freezing," I said.

That's when Amanda tugged me on the arm, threw me a mischievous look, and said, "Presenting Megan Murray and Amanda Harding singing their version of 'Deck the Halls.' " She threw her head back and started singing. "Deck the halls with boughs of holly . . ."

What was I going to do? I had to join in. "Fa-la-la-la-la . . ." I fell into the harmony we had learned in chorus.

Now, you have to understand, I don't usually sing in the streets. I'm a basically quiet person. Some people might even call me shy. But Amanda had a way of bringing out a different side of me. Maybe that's why she was my favorite person in the entire world.

We had been best friends since fourth grade. I could tell Amanda absolutely anything I was feeling or thinking.

Anyway, after shopping, her mom drove me all the way back to Greatdale. When I waved good-bye and ran to my house I was in a really great mood. I had spent my entire savings on Christmas gifts, but I'd gotten some really neat presents. Like I said, life was pretty perfect.

"Hi, sweetheart," my mother called out from her office off our front hallway. As usual, she was in front of the computer with a pencil tucked up in her tumbling-down, light-brown bun. She does bookkeeping for a few local businesses.

"Hi, Mom," I said, dashing up to my room. I wanted to get the presents wrapped before she got curious about them.

Just as I finished wrapping the book of poetry I'd bought for my dad, I heard his car pull into the driveway. He was beeping the horn like crazy.

That was weird. You see, my dad is a quiet, laid-back kind of guy. If he was honking his horn, there had to be a good reason. I went to the window and watched him emerge from the car with a giant bouquet. He had a huge grin on his face.

What in the world was going on? I raced downstairs to find out.

Mom was already at the door, hugging him. My parents can be pretty lovey-dovey at times. When they overdo it, it's gross, but mostly it's kind of cute.

"Oh, Paul!" she said. "I'm so proud!"

Then they broke apart and started jumping up and down like little kids.

"Hey, what's going on?" I asked.

Dad let out a laugh, and reached over to give me a hug. "Wait till you hear, my Little Bunsen Burner!" he said.

Don't tell me. I already know. Little Bunsen Burner has got to be the dumbest nickname a kid ever had. Dad started calling me that when I was little—because he's a scientist, and I used to have bright red hair. Now my hair is more brown than red, but he still comes out with the old nickname when he's excited about something.

"I got the job at Colton College!" he blurted out. He and Mom started whooping it up again.

"Cool," I said. Colton College has a great reputation, and I knew it was my dad's dream to teach there. "That's great, Dad. Are you going to be making a lot more money?" I asked.

He grinned and cleared his throat. "Not very much more, actually."

"But he'll have much more academic freedom." Mom was talking to me, but her eyes were fixed on Dad. "Isn't it wonderful?"

"Fantastic," I agreed. "Here, give me those flowers. I'll put them in water."

Dad's face clouded over. He gave Mom

another squeeze around the shoulders and nodded at her.

"I'll take care of the flowers, honey," Mom said softly. She disappeared into the kitchen as my dad steered me into the living room.

I guess that was when the first alarm bell started ringing somewhere in the back of my head.

Dad motioned for me to sit down. "Megan, you know you're on a special scholarship, just for children of Mead employees."

"Of course," I said. "What about it?"

"Well, Megan, Mead Academy is a tremendously expensive school." His voice was pinched and he looked like he had a headache. "Now that I won't be teaching there anymore—"

My throat went dry. "You're not going to tell me I have to leave Mead, are you?"

"Yes, I'm afraid so, honey."

This could not be happening. I kept waiting for him to smile and tell me it was all a joke.

"After the break, you'll be transferring to Midway Junior High," he said with a sigh.

"Midway?" I said, dumbstruck. I knew Midway. It was a public school not far from our house. But he was wrong. I wasn't going to transfer there, not for the world. I loved going to Mead Academy!

"Believe me," he said softly. "I wish you could have finished out the term at Mead."

"But I can," I pointed out. "If you can't afford it, I'll get a job and pay for it myself."

"Honey, a term at Mead costs thousands of dollars," Dad said.

"So what?" I countered. "I'll lie about my age so I can work every night. And I'll work weekends, too. And in my spare time, I can baby-sit."

"No, Megan," he said, shaking his head. "I'm afraid the only way we could swing it would be to rob your college fund."

"Go ahead! Rob it!" I said desperately. "I think that's a great idea!"

"Honey, it's a terrible idea and you know it," he said. "You're going to need that money in just four years."

I couldn't really argue with him about that, so I just leaned back on the sofa and tried to calm down. I was having trouble breathing. I think my heart had stopped.

"You know something, Meggie?" he said, trying to put on a smile. "I'll bet if you give Midway a chance, you might find out that—"

The last thing I wanted at that moment was a pep talk. "Dad, please," I said.

"Midway has a terrific science program, *and* a lot of extracurricular activities—more than

Mead, in fact. They have chess and a nature club—"

"Dad, stop!" I broke in angrily. "I don't care how many clubs they have!" I pounded my fists on my knees. "I don't know anybody there! Not one kid!"

"You know Kevin MacArthur," he pointed out. Kevin's parents and my parents are close friends, so I had known Kevin for a long time. He was a nice kid, but he wasn't exactly best friend material.

"Kevin's a *boy*!" I yelled, as if being a boy meant he was subhuman.

My dad let out a heavy sigh and squeezed his eyes shut. At that moment, the rest of the truth hit me.

There were boys at Midway!

Mead is an all-girl school. The last time I'd gone to school with boys was in third grade! Besides Kevin, the only boys I knew were Jim and Corey Parker from down the block, and I didn't know them very well.

"I'm sure you'll make lots of new friends at Midway—boys as well as girls," Dad said.

"I don't want new friends," I wailed. "I'm happy with my old ones. If I stop going to Mead, I'll never see Amanda anymore."

I wasn't really trying to sound whiny. It just came out that way.

"Of course you'll see her," my dad said.

How could I believe him? Meadsville was almost an hour away. My parents and Amanda's parents were too busy to ferry us back and forth.

Dad reached for my hand. "Honey, Mom and I have gone over the numbers a hundred times, and it's just got to be. The sooner you accept it, the better. If you can manage to look at the bright side—"

He babbled on and on, trying to make me feel better. I listened as long as I could, then I pulled my hand away and screamed, "Forget it! I'm not going! And you can't make me!"

Bolting from the living room, I ran upstairs. I didn't stop until I was in my room with the door safely slammed behind me.

Part of me wanted to call Amanda right away. But I was much too upset to talk to anyone. Besides, how was I ever going to tell her such bad news? She'd be as devastated as I was!

I threw myself on the bed and gazed up at the ceiling. I was trying not to cry when I heard a soft knock on my door. My mom poked her head in. "Are you okay, honey?"

"I'm fine," I tried to say. But it must have come out more like "Boo-hoo" or something, because she rushed right over to me and held me in her arms. I bit my lip real hard so she wouldn't see how I felt. I certainly was not about to share my deepest feelings with a traitor like her.

"Come on, Megan, it won't be so bad," she said in a soothing voice.

I sat up on the edge of the bed and took a deep breath. "Oh, sure, sure."

"Kevin's parents told us Midway's won several awards, you know."

"Who cares," I mumbled.

"And just think," my mom went on, ignoring me, as she touched the strap of my Mead jumper. "You'll never have to wear this *gorgeous* uniform again."

I couldn't help smiling at her sarcasm. The plaid Mead jumper, with its patches of olive green and maroon, had to be the most hideous outfit in the entire universe.

"Aha!" she said with a laugh. "I got you there!" She gave me a squeeze around the shoulders. "Tell you what—after the holiday, we'll go shopping and buy you a bunch of new clothes. What do you say?"

Actually, that sounded pretty good. "Okay," I mumbled.

"Feeling better?"

"A little," I said.

"Well, come down when you get hungry." She gave my shoulders one last squeeze before she got up to go.

After she left, I sat on my bed and tried to calm down. True, my life was taking a pretty sharp turn, but maybe everything would work out. In a small secret part of myself, I had always wondered what public school was like. Even the idea of going to school with boys was more intriguing than it was scary.

I pulled a tissue from my pocket and blew my nose. Maybe when I got used to the idea of switching schools I might even be excited about it. Midway could turn out to be fun. And like Mom had said, I would never have to wear that ugly Mead uniform again.

I stood up and walked over to the mirror on my closet door. The uniform really *was* a horror story. But oh, what wonderful times I'd had in it! Now that whole part of me, the best part, was gone. Just like that.

Suddenly, I started sobbing again. Tears poured all over that ugly Mead uniform—the dearest, most wonderful thing I had ever worn.

CHAPTER

By the end of the week, I had prepared myself to see Amanda. My dad was driving to Mead to clean out his desk, so it was the perfect time to get a ride.

When I called Amanda and asked if I could come over, though, I didn't say anything was wrong. I knew I had to do that in person.

Soon I was on the Hardings' porch, pressing the doorbell and trying to force a holiday smile onto my face. Of course, that didn't fool Amanda.

"Yikes, Megan!" she said, the minute she opened the door. "What's wrong?"

I wasn't ready to drop the bomb just yet.

"Oh, I'm just in a bad mood, that's all," I said. I walked in and took off my coat.

Amanda flashed me a sneaky grin. "Well, maybe this will cheer you up." She walked over to the tree in her living room, reached down for a silver-wrapped box, and tossed it to me. "Merry Christmas, Scrooge."

It's really hard to be sad around Amanda. But this time, even the little laugh that came out of me hurt.

"Come on, open it. Open it!" she said, moving her arms around like an orchestra leader. "It's for when we have our debate with Frick."

Frick was another all-girl school. The two schools had been rivals since the Stone Age. But recently, Frick had announced it was going co-ed.

I opened the box and pulled out a green T-shirt with maroon writing. It read: MEAD ACADEMY: ALL-GIRL AND PROUD OF IT. "Cool, huh?" Amanda said, with a laugh.

My hands were shaking. "Thanks," I said. "It's really cute."

Amanda's face clouded over. "Megan, what in the world is wrong?" she asked.

"I'm not coming back to Mead, Mandy," I blurted out. I wanted to be mature and everything, but this stupid tear started rolling down my cheek.

She was absolutely stunned. "What are you talking about?"

I explained the whole miserable situation to her—how I had to go to Midway from now on, and why. As she listened, her face started crumpling up like a used candy wrapper.

"I don't believe this," Amanda kept saying. "I mean, this is truly unbelievable."

"I know," I said.

Then we both sat there, not saying much, for a really long time.

"Wait!" she said. "What are we getting all upset about, anyway? We're still going to be friends—that's forever! Right?" She had her hands on her hips and she sounded real definite.

"Right!" I agreed, trying to match her confidence.

"So what's the big deal if we don't go to the same school? That doesn't make any difference to us. Right?"

"Right!" I agreed. "The important thing is that we're both on the same planet. Right?"

"The same planet?" she said with a giggle. "Megan, you're too much." Then she brushed away a tear of her own. "Okay, now I want to hear all about the new school you're going to. Tell me everything you know."

"I don't know that much about it, really," I began. "Just that there are boys—"

"Boys! That's great!" Amanda shrieked. "Oh, you're so lucky! I wish Mead had boys."

I looked down at the T-shirt she'd just given me—ALL-GIRL AND PROUD OF IT—and I wondered if she was saying that about boys just to cheer me up. "It's supposed to be pretty good in science, too," I said, trying to get off the uncomfortable subject of boys. But just then, my dad pulled into the driveway and tooted his horn. "Oh, no. I have to go," I cried.

"Wait! When will I see you?" she asked, sounding a little shaky.

"Real soon," I told her. "I'll get my mom to drive me over."

"Me, too. I'll get mine to take me to Greatdale," she said. "And I'll call you."

"Me, too," I said. "A lot."

We gave each other a big hug. Then I grabbed my coat and ran out of her house, feeling worse than ever. Now there were *two* miserable people in this world—me and Amanda.

"Hi, honey," my dad said. "Did you have a nice time?"

What a dumb question. I was too mad to say anything, so I just ignored him and stared out the passenger window the whole way home. I figured that was the least he deserved.

*　　*　　*

22

You can imagine what Christmas was like. All the relatives made a big fuss about Dad's new job. They kept calling him "Professor," and stuff like that. Mom kept giving him these adoring looks, which he ate up. Obviously, they were too wrapped up in themselves to think about my feelings.

"So, Megan, are you excited about going to a new school?" my grandmother asked me during Christmas dinner.

I didn't want to go into it with her so I just shrugged. "I guess so, Gram," I fibbed.

"Well, I think it will be much better for you. That other place was too snooty."

That's how much she knew. It really kills me how grownups, even basically nice ones like Gram, think they know so much more about your life than you do.

After dessert, we opened presents in the living room. Gram gave me a new Walkman, which was a cool gift. From my parents I got a card telling me that I was a wonderful daughter and that they were sure I would do fine at Midway. Their present was a gift-wrapped fashion magazine with an IOU taped on it. It said, "We owe you one shopping spree. Love, Mom and Dad."

I thanked everybody, then disappeared into my room while the grownups talked. So much for Christmas cheer.

In fact, I spent a lot of time in my room over that holiday. I could tell my parents were concerned, but they didn't want to butt in. That was just fine with me.

One morning I was lying in bed deciding whether to get up or not, when my mother walked in. Without knocking.

"Oops," she said, tapping the door after she was already halfway through it. "Can I come in?" It was a little late to ask permission, so I didn't say anything.

"I'm all ready," she said cheerfully. "How much time do you need?"

"What do you mean?" I mumbled.

"We're going shopping, remember?"

I got dressed, and about thirty minutes later we were on our way to the mall. To tell you the truth, I was pretty excited by the time we got there. Greatdale Mall is a really awesome place. It has huge skylights and a terrific Food Court.

"I think it's important to buy things that go together," Mom said the minute we stepped on the escalator. "We'll start at Hogan's. They'll be having a good sale. We can get shoes at Shoe-O-Rama."

Obviously, Mom had everything worked out, which irritated me a little. Wasn't this trip supposed to be for me?

We looked for skirts right away. Everything

24

had a tag that said: No Returns on Sale Items. Before I knew it, my mother had picked out some navy and gray skirts for me to try on.

"Those are boring!" I said.

"Megan, they're basics," she said. "If you start with neutral colors you'll be able to build your new wardrobe."

I don't know why I didn't argue with her, but I certainly should have. I guess I didn't want to seem ungrateful. After all, she was spending a bundle of money on me.

By noon, we were loaded down with bags full of "basics." I tried to pick out clothes that were really cool, but my mother didn't like any of my suggestions.

"Not made well," she said when I showed her a neat sweatshirt with lace sewn onto it.

"Too intense," she murmured when I held up a pair of purple leggings.

"Too casual," she said when I picked out a denim shirt with studs on the front.

But the worst part was when we went to Shoe-O-Rama. I actually let her talk me into buying a pair of clunky navy blue loafers that were on sale.

"What a price for genuine leather," my mother said, looking down at my feet. "And they'll match everything we bought today. How do they feel?"

I wanted to lie, but I couldn't. "They feel okay," I mumbled.

The next thing I knew, we were standing at the cashier's counter paying for the shoes. "Finally! We're all done!" Mom said, after she handed the clerk her credit card.

Mom looked as exhausted as I felt. "Let's go get something to drink," I suggested.

"That's a great idea," Mom said.

We went up one level to the Food Court. Mom sat at a table while I ordered two fruit smoothies at a frozen yogurt stand. When I brought them over to the table, Mom was busy talking to a woman she used to work with.

"Megan, this is Frances Connor," she said.

Ms. Connor and I nodded, and they started catching up on old times while I just sort of looked around. Soon a group of girls my age came in at the other side of the Court. They were all wearing purple and gold Midway jackets.

I couldn't believe how gorgeous these girls were—especially one dark-haired girl. She looked more like an actress or a movie star than a junior high student.

She and her friends were giggling and pointing at a group of good-looking boys sitting at the table near them.

The girls had a lot of make-up on, but it

looked great. At Mead, make-up was strictly forbidden, even for the seniors.

The only time I got to wear make-up was on super-special occasions. My parents wanted me to wait until I was fifteen to wear it every day.

As for their clothes, these girls had things that looked great, but really comfortable, too. Most of them wore leggings or tights with big sweatshirts and ankle boots. When they'd bought their clothes, they obviously hadn't shopped for "basics."

I sank down into my seat and slurped up my smoothie. Just looking at the kids I'd be going to school with had made me totally depressed.

My first day at Midway was only three days away. And I was going to show up there looking like a total dweeb!

CHAPTER

3

I could hardly wait to see Kevin MacArthur when his family came over on New Year's Eve. Spending New Year's Eve together was a tradition for our parents that had started when they were college students. When we were younger, Kevin and I would play. For the last few years, though, we would watch a movie or play chess.

Like I said, Kevin was a nice kid, but I certainly didn't think of him as a good friend. Still, this year, I couldn't wait to pump him for information about Midway.

The minute the MacArthurs arrived, I asked Kevin if he wanted to go outside for a while.

There was snow on the ground, but it wasn't that cold out.

"So, are you excited about going back to school?" I asked as soon as we were out. Maybe it was a leading question. But I wanted to know how Kevin really felt about Midway.

Kevin walked over to a big lump of snow that had fallen off our maple tree. "Why would I be excited about going back to school?" he asked, picking up some snow and pressing it onto the lump. He sounded like he thought I was nuts.

My heart sank. "I was just wondering," I mumbled. I shoved some more snow onto the pile. "Actually, I'm going to be transferring there."

"Oh, right," Kevin said, looking embarrassed. "My mom told me, but I forgot. Well, you'll like Midway. It's not that bad." He went back to pushing snow on the lump.

"Not that bad" wasn't exactly the description I wanted to hear.

"They've got a shortwave radio club, and a chess club, too. I'm in both."

I didn't know the first thing about shortwave radios, but I was in the chess club at Mead. "Who's in the chess club?"

"Let's see," Kevin pondered. "There's me, Elliott Wasserman, Joseph Truro, Andrew Sender, and Alan Darwib."

Terrific. All boys.

"Elliott Wasserman is my best friend," Kevin said, pushing his glasses back up on his nose. There was a big wad of masking tape holding them together right in the middle over his nose.

Somebody should tell him to get a new pair, I thought. But I wasn't good enough friends with him to say something like that.

"Kids!" my mother shouted from the kitchen window. "There'll be some hot chocolate ready in a few minutes."

I nodded, and Kevin said, "Great!" Then he looked at the snow we'd been pushing around. It had the distinct shape of a snowman. "Pretty good," he said, with a grin. "Imagine what we could do if we'd put our minds to it."

We started walking toward the house. "What are the girls like?" I asked.

Kevin stuck his gloved hands in his pockets and shrugged. "Some of them are real jerks. They give me a hard time about my height. I just don't pay any attention to them."

I got the feeling that Kevin paid plenty of attention to what they said. He looked miserable.

"Hey, like you say, they're just jerks," I said. "And besides, you're getting taller. I noticed when you first came over."

That got him. He stopped and broke out in

a big smile. "I grew two inches this year. My dad says I'm probably starting my growth spurt."

"I'll bet you are," I said, nodding.

"You think so?" He was staring at me, straight in the eye, with this worried kind of look.

I turned away. How did I know? "I'm getting cold. Let's go inside, okay?" Everything Kevin had said about Midway had me feeling really terrible.

Kevin must have realized that, too, because when we were finishing our hot chocolate he said, "Listen, Megan, Midway's really a pretty neat school. I bet you'll really like it."

"Okay," I said. It wasn't the greatest response, but I couldn't think of a better one.

"I mean, it's different with me. I kind of have a reputation for being a brain, you know, a nerd or something."

"Oh?" I said. I was a little surprised by his confession, and I didn't know how to respond.

"Being a brain at Midway is kind of like being a dummy someplace else, know what I mean?" Kevin shrugged and took a big gulp of hot chocolate.

I just stared at him. If he was trying to make me feel better, he definitely had not succeeded. After all, I was a "brain," too. *Everyone* at Mead was a brain.

I made a mental note. When I got to Midway

I was going to do two things. The first was to act real "cool," like I had a fascinating personality. The second was to act dumb, so kids wouldn't think I was a brain.

Maybe it wasn't the greatest plan in the world, but at least it was a plan.

"What movie did you bring?" I asked.

"*Revenge of the Alien Computer*," Kevin told me with a big smile. "But we don't have to watch it if you don't want to."

"Oh, no, it's okay," I said. What difference did it make? My life was over anyway.

Actually, the movie didn't turn out to be that bad, but I still couldn't get into it. I was too busy being depressed.

When midnight came, our parents walked into the den, blowing noisemakers and screaming "Happy New Year!"

"I hope this year is the best ever for you, Megan," my mom said.

"Hear! Hear!" Dad said. "Happy New Year!"

I gritted my teeth and let them hug me. "To you, too," I said. But what I felt like saying wouldn't have sounded so nice.

I called Amanda the night before school started. "Tomorrow's the big day," I said with a sigh.

"I know," she said, quietly. "How are you feeling?"

"Terrified," I said. "I don't know which is worse: thinking they'll all stare at me, or thinking they'll ignore me."

"It doesn't have to be one way or the other, you know," she said, with a laugh. "Maybe they'll stare at you *and* ignore you."

I laughed. I already felt a hundred times better just talking to Amanda. "If only you were going to be there."

"Mead is going to feel so empty without you." I thought I heard a catch in her voice, like she was about to cry. "Hey! Let's get together on Saturday, okay?"

"Definitely," I said. "My parents owe me that much."

"Come on, Megan," Amanda cautioned me. "They're just doing what they think is best for the whole family."

I felt a little annoyed. "You sound just like them."

"Well, it's true, if you think about it, Megan. They aren't sending you to Midway just to be mean. And you know what?" she added, brightening. "I bet you'll be a smash hit there."

"Yeah, right," I said. "That'll be the day. I sure do sparkle, don't I? Especially when I'm scared." I pretended to be reading a newspaper headline. " 'Frozen With Fear, Mead Girl Wows Public School Kids With Perfect Mummy Imitation.' "

"Stop," Amanda said, her voice softening. "It'll take time, but it'll happen. By the end of the term, I'll be saying 'I told you so.' You wait and see."

That's why Amanda is so great. She keeps at you relentlessly until you just have to give in and feel better.

I thought I would be up all night, but I actually got a good night's sleep. I guess talking to Amanda calmed me down.

Then it was morning, and there was no time to think. I got dressed in the navy skirt and a pale blue blouse, which was about the wildest combination of my new clothes. I wished I could put on a little lipstick, but I didn't want to upset my parents. The last thing I needed that morning was trouble from them.

"Megan, would you like me to drive you to school?" my mom asked as I finished my cereal.

"Thanks," I said. "That would be great." True, Midway is only six blocks from our house, and I could have walked there. But it was freezing cold that day.

On the way over to school, Mom was quiet. But when I started to get out of the car, she reached over and touched me on the arm. "Megan," she said, "I know you're scared. But I promise you, everything will work out just fine." I knew she was trying to sound positive, but it came out tense.

"Thanks, Mom," I told her. I didn't want to argue with her. Of course, the real truth was she couldn't promise me anything. Today, I was on my own.

When the car pulled away, I turned around and took a good look at Midway Junior High. It was huge. I gathered every ounce of courage in me, and, with the freezing wind blowing straight into my face, I plodded up the steps and went inside.

As I opened the door, a blast of hot air hit me. The hall was filled with thousands of kids—well, hundreds, anyway. They were huddled in groups, talking a million miles an hour. They all seemed happy and excited to be with each other. Most of them were wearing casual clothes, like sweaters and jeans. None of the girls wore skirts.

A few kids glanced at me, then turned away. The way I was dressed, they probably thought I had blown in from a time warp.

I found the office easily enough. "Hi," I said to a young red-haired woman who was busily stamping a stack of papers. "I'm new. My name is Megan Murray."

The woman didn't even glance up at me. "See Mrs. Cook, not me," she murmured grouchily as she continued her work.

Who was Mrs. Cook? I didn't have a clue.

Fortunately, a friendly man with a neatly trimmed dark beard walked up to me and said, "Mrs. Cook will be right back. There's her desk." He pointed to a desk across the room.

"Thanks," I told him.

I walked over to Mrs. Cook's desk just as a blonde woman with hoop earrings came into the office.

"Mrs. Cook," the man said, "you have a customer."

"Don't tell me," Mrs. Cook said, smiling at me as she picked up a large yellow card from her desk. "You're Megan Murray."

"Right," I said, surprised. "How did you know?"

"I'm psychic," Mrs. Cook said with a grin as she handed me the card. "Also, they sent a photo of you from Mead. Here's your schedule, Megan. If you have any problems, let us know."

Maybe Midway was going to be okay, I thought as I watched her disappear into another office. Then I checked my schedule. My homeroom was Room 214. Where was that?

I would have asked the red-haired woman, but she didn't look like she wanted to be bothered.

Besides, Megan, I told myself, you're a big girl, not a baby.

I walked out of the office into the hallway and started looking for the stairs. On every side of me were those strange creatures, the ones we didn't have at Mead: boys. They were all different heights and weights, but they were all *loud*.

I made my way through the crowd and finally found a stairwell marked "B Stairs." There, I told myself, you're doing just fine. But when I got to the first landing, I wanted to sink down into the ground and disappear. A boy and girl were standing in the stairwell, *kissing*.

As soon as they heard me coming, they quickly broke apart. I don't know which of us was more embarrassed, but I think it was me.

Blushing like crazy, I put my head down and hurried up the stairs. I ran straight into this big guy who was coming down the stairs.

"Hey! Look where you're going," he yelled. He looked closely at me and said, "Nice shoes." Then he laughed and continued down the stairs.

Suddenly, those new shoes of mine looked exactly like the ones the Pilgrim fathers wore when they first landed at Plymouth Rock.

Day one at Midway had just begun.

So far, not so good.

CHAPTER

Once I got to the second floor hallway, I checked my watch. There were twelve minutes left before the bell. I figured I would find my locker and make it to my homeroom a little early.

Except I didn't get there early. What I got was lost.

Midway Junior High is built like a giant letter "L." But there are all these little hallways going off the "L" shape. It's like an "L" with bumps. I found Rooms 205 to 212 in one of the bumps. I found Rooms 217 to 224 in another. But where was 214?

Trying not to panic, I stopped in the middle of the hallway and just stood there. Being lost was a new sensation for me. Usually, I have a great sense of direction.

Kids were rushing past me every half second. When I heard the bell, I nearly jumped two feet in the air. It sounded like a clanging fire alarm, not like the gentle chimes they used at Mead.

Just then, I felt a hand on my shoulder. I let out a scream.

"Hey, take it easy! It's only me, not Count Dracula."

I spun around and found myself looking into Kevin MacArthur's hazel eyes. He still had masking tape wrapped around his glasses.

"Kevin, I'm lost," I explained, hoping my embarrassment didn't show too badly. "Where in the world is Room 214, anyway?"

"It's right behind you, Megan," Kevin answered. He didn't laugh, which was nice of him. "In fact, that's my homeroom, too," he said with a smile.

I can't tell you how relieved I felt when he said that. I followed him into the room and we sat down next to each other, over near the windows. "Let's see your schedule," he said, holding out his hand for it.

I gave him the yellow card, and he looked it over. "We don't have any other classes together," he said, shaking his head and handing the card back to me. "Oh, well."

"What about lunch?" I asked, sounding a little nervous.

"This is a big school," he replied. "There are two different lunch periods. I'm in B and you're in A."

Two lunch periods? That was weird. At Mead, everyone always had lunch together. It was one of the highlights of the day.

Just then, a teacher walked in. He was the same man who had helped me down in the office.

"Mr. Barrazutti!" one of the kids shouted.

"Hey, guys! How was the break? I bet you missed me terribly," the teacher joked.

Everyone laughed, and I smiled. Mr. Barrazutti seemed really nice.

"People, say hello to Megan Murray. She's a new student here," he announced, pointing in my direction. The other kids all turned and looked at me curiously. A few murmured, "Hi," but without much enthusiasm. My cheeks started getting hot as I nodded back to them. But fortunately, Mr. Barrazutti began making some announcements. A few minutes later, the bell clanged again.

Kevin's next class was Spanish. He said it was in the same direction as my first class, biology, so he walked me there. I was glad about that. Getting lost again would have been too humiliating for words.

"There's the biology room," Kevin said, pointing to Room 240. I stopped short. Standing in front of the door were the same girls I had seen at the mall. The one with the glossy black hair and wide dark eyes seemed to be the center of attention. The other girls were just standing around, listening to her talk.

Wouldn't it be neat to be popular like that, I thought. This girl was really pretty. She had lipstick and eye make-up on, and she was wearing a cool black top with padded shoulders and a scoop neck.

"That's Rosemary Weil, holding court," Kevin mumbled in my ear. "I guess you could say she's Midway's reigning status queen."

I wasn't sure what that meant, but I couldn't take my eyes off Rosemary.

"She's so pretty," I said.

"Yeah? Well, looks can be deceiving," Kevin said sourly. "Remember I told you about some girls teasing me about my height?" He rolled his eyes in Rosemary's direction. "Be prepared," he warned me, and shuffled off to his Spanish class.

Once Kevin walked away, I tried to look cool by keeping my face set in a neutral position. My big act of courage was to give the Midway girls a nod when I walked in.

They looked at me as if to say, "Who's she?"

Remembering to keep my back straight, I walked past them.

That's when I heard the giggles. I told myself not to be paranoid. But I have to admit the bottom dropped right out of my stomach for a minute.

"Hi, I'm Ms. Cornwall," the teacher said when I walked into the classroom. She was wearing a dark red skirt with a matching vest and scarf. "Welcome to Midway."

"Thanks," I said. "I'm Megan Murray."

"That's a very pretty name," she said. "Why don't you take a seat over there, Megan?" She pointed to an empty seat in the back row. I went over to it and sat down.

"Let's go, class. We don't have time to waste," Ms. Cornwall told the students who were still getting settled. "We have a lot of work to cover today."

I glanced around the room and noticed Rosemary sitting a few rows in front of me. She had a small mirror in her lap, and was checking her make-up.

"Okay, class," Ms. Cornwall began. "Let's review our work from before the vacation. Who can tell me the name of the process by which water molecules cross a cell's membrane?"

Like I said, science is my best subject. But still, I couldn't believe my ears. Ms. Cornwall was teaching stuff I'd learned in the eighth grade at Mead.

Still, nobody raised a hand to answer.

"Come on, people, you should know this," she said.

One or two hands shot up, but Ms. Cornwall didn't call on those kids. Instead she called on Rosemary Weil.

"Rosemary?" she urged.

Rosemary quickly slid her make-up mirror into her knapsack. Then she tilted her head to one side. "Um, is it diffusion?" she guessed.

Ms. Cornwall shook her head and let out a sigh. "No, it's not. David Paul Ehrlich? Can you help me out?"

A boy who was sitting in the front row shrugged his shoulders. "The process by which water molecules pass through a cell's membrane . . . ? Sorry, Ms. Cornwall," he said.

Now I realized how great a school Mead was. Every kid at Mead would have known the answer to a simple question like that.

Still, I wasn't about to raise my hand to volunteer the answer. The last thing I wanted at Midway was a reputation as a "brain."

Then, to my horror, Ms. Cornwall's eyes zoomed in straight at me. "How about you, Megan?" she asked. "Can you enlighten us?"

For a split second, I didn't know what to do.

But before I knew it, my big mouth opened up and the answer popped out. "It's osmosis," I said.

"Very good," Ms. Cornwall said with a smile. "But maybe we should double back for a minute. Let's go back to the basic unit of life— the cell. What are the chemical components of a cell?"

This time the teacher called on Farrah, one of Rosemary's friends, who sat in the front row. "Water?" Farrah said, more like a question than an answer.

"No," Ms. Cornwall told her. "Rosemary, is your hand up?"

Rosemary looked flustered. "No, I was just fixing my hair," she murmured.

"Could you please save that for after class?" the teacher said. "Come on, people. I'm looking for the basic components of a cell. Megan? Maybe you can help us out again?"

"Well," I said with a gulp. "There's nucleic acid."

"Yes?" Ms. Cornwall encouraged. "And what else?"

"Well, um, protein," I murmured, looking up at the teacher. She seemed so interested in what I was saying, like she was silently urging me on. "Also, carbohydrates, lipids, and inorganic ions."

A big "Whoa!" went up from the kids in the

class. Rats! Why couldn't I have kept my mouth shut? Now everyone was staring at me. It felt like they were all looking at my huge, oversized brain.

"Excellent!" Ms. Cornwall said. "I see we have a biology expert on our hands! That's just what we need around here!"

The teacher looked tremendously pleased. I, on the other hand, could not have been more miserable.

Biology was followed by English, which was followed by math. Math, thank goodness, was followed by *lunch*. I couldn't believe I had three heavy classes one after the other. I had been given an incredible amount of homework to do for the next day. Not that it was anything hard. It was basically the same stuff we'd done at Mead back in the fall. Still, it was going to be a long, boring evening.

I put my math book into my bag and headed out into the hall. Other kids brushed past me, talking with their friends and sharing "in" jokes and gossip. This was the time Amanda and I would be making plans, cooking up something fun for after school. I felt like crying right there in the hall, but I managed to get a hold of myself in time.

The cafeteria at Midway was the size of a

football field, and the noise was unbelievable. It made the Mead cafeteria seem like a nice, quiet restaurant.

Fortunately, the food didn't look too bad. Not that it mattered that day; I was much too nervous to eat. My stomach was doing flip-flops as I took my tray and started looking for a place to sit. In class you have an excuse for not talking to people—you just pay attention to the teacher. But in the cafeteria, you'd have to be a complete reject not to talk to *somebody*. I mean, there had to be hundreds of kids there.

Most of the tables were full, but there were a few empty spaces to sit here and there. The trouble was, you practically had to sit down right in the middle of somebody else's conversation. That would be totally uncool.

I kept moving, looking for the right place to sit. I was careful not to bump into people and spill my chicken a la king all over myself, or them.

Then I saw Rosemary Weil and her friends. For a minute I considered walking over to their table and asking if I could sit there. Rosemary might be the most popular girl in the school, but I did have a class with her. I took a few steps toward the table, but then I lost my courage. Suddenly, I felt completely self-conscious.

I just couldn't bring myself to barge right in and ask to sit with them. If they said no or laughed at me, I'd have just died, right there in the cafeteria.

So instead, I pretended I heard someone calling me. I darted off in the other direction.

I was over by the far exit now. There were more free spaces here—even a few empty tables. By this point, I was ready to give up and eat lunch alone.

A vivid picture of the Mead cafeteria came into my mind—Charlie the cook, Myrtle and Barbara, the women who served the food, the green and white curtains. Suddenly I missed them so badly it hurt.

"Hi," came a voice on my right as I sat down at one of the empty tables. "You want some company?"

I turned around and saw this really pretty black girl with thick, wavy hair and dark eyes. She was wearing a Midway cheerleader's sweater with the name Terri on it.

"Sure," I mumbled.

"I'm Terri Lawson," she said, dropping her tray across from mine on the table.

"I'm Megan," I said, firmly. "Megan Murray. I'm new here."

"Neat!" she said, plopping down across from me. "That's what this school needs—some new blood."

47

"New victims, you mean?" I said. It was a pretty feeble joke, but Terri laughed at it.

"Right. So, how do you like it so far?" She had ordered the fish, and she was cutting it up as she talked. Obviously, she was as at home here as if it were her own kitchen.

"It's okay, I guess," I said, shrugging. I poked at my food a little bit. The peas were bright kelly green.

"It must be hard," she said. She stopped eating for a minute and stared into space. "If it were me, I think I'd be terrified."

A relieved laugh just popped out of me when she said that. I couldn't believe this girl, this total stranger, had read my mind so perfectly. "Terrified, petrified, mortified, take your pick," I admitted, laughing again.

"It's just natural, I guess," Terri said. "You could think of it this way, though. It will all be over in six months and then we'll all be on our way to high school, right?" She winked, and went back to eating. "No, seriously, Megan, you'll like Midway. Just hang in there. Even if it takes a while, this place is really pretty good, once you get to know it."

I had just one thought running through my head, over and over again. I hoped Terri could read my mind as well as she had a minute ago: BE MY FRIEND, BE MY FRIEND, BE MY FRIEND . . .

But I couldn't just come out and say it. That would have been totally embarrassing. Besides, this girl probably had a thousand friends. She was nice, and a cheerleader.

So I didn't say anything. We just ate for another minute or so, and then she called out, "Hi, Frank."

A big hunk of a guy came ambling over, holding his tray. There were two other boys behind him. Frank walked up to the table and sat down next to Terri. One of the other boys sat next to Frank, and the other next to me.

"How did it go this weekend?" Terri asked Frank.

"Uh, not too good, actually," he answered. I didn't know what they were talking about, and I guess I wasn't supposed to, so I just kept eating. "Can we go talk over there?" he asked her, nodding to another table.

"Sure," Terri said. She turned to me and smiled regretfully. "Nice meeting you, Megan." Then she got up and turned to the other two boys. "Ira, Curtis, this is Megan. Behave yourselves, okay?" She waved at me as she walked off with Frank.

So there I was, suddenly alone with two boys. My heart was racing with fear. What was I going to say to them?

Fortunately, I didn't have to worry. As far as

Ira and Curtis were concerned, I might as well have been part of the furniture.

"Hey, Curtis, where'd you get those new sneakers?" Ira said, snorting and showing his teeth. They were covered with braces which were covered with crud. "They look like clown shoes, man."

Curtis would have been okay-looking if it weren't for his skin. His face must have really hurt, with all those pimples on it. "Eat my socks, Miller," he said. "You wish you had 'em."

"Yeah, I'll trade you my old underwear for 'em, okay?" said Ira. I rolled my eyes. Frank seemed to be okay, but these two guys were total geeks.

Then they started shooting straw wrappers at one another in rapid fire. I decided I had better go before I found myself in the middle of a full-fledged food fight.

Dumping my tray on the tray rack, I crashed through the exit doors and ran up the stairs. I had to calm down before I lost it altogether.

That cafeteria is a zoo, I thought to myself. In fact, Midway Junior High was the loneliest, grossest, most horrible place on earth!

CHAPTER

Somehow I got through the afternoon, even though my left shoe had rubbed a huge blister into my heel. Fortunately, I could still walk without wobbling. The last thing I needed was a limp.

The best part of Midway turned out to be the classes. Once I got a feeling for how the building was laid out, I made my way around fairly easily. And it was sort of fun having more kids in the classes. At Mead, each class had about ten girls. Here, there were over twenty kids in each class, so it was easier to blend in and disappear.

French was fun, since I'd been studying it since the fifth grade. The Midway teacher, Mr.

DeHais, was a native speaker who told lots of good stories about when he lived in Paris. He was a balding man who wore a small bow tie. His class seemed to speed by, thanks to his funny stories, all told in simple French, of course.

In social studies, we were doing a unit on Appalachia. The teacher, Ms. Lin, had a display of hand-crafted goods from the area, which I thought was neat. One of Rosemary's friends, a girl named Heather, had the seat next to mine. She was blond-haired, and she wore a Matt Springer T-shirt under her black leather vest. I didn't nod or say hello or anything. But at one point, when the teacher asked the class to get out their textbooks, she mumbled, "Appalachia—ick. Poor people are so boring."

I wasn't sure if she was talking to me, so I didn't say anything back. I just gave a little shrug.

Then there was chorus, with a whole new group of kids I hadn't seen before. Thankfully, the boys sat on one side of the platform and the girls on the other. I was scared that if I had to share my music with a boy I might do something really dumb.

Mrs. Friedman, the chorus leader, was an overweight, cheerful woman of about fifty.

"Hello, Megan," she said, shaking my hand. "Are you an alto or soprano?"

"Alto," I told her.

"There's your section," she said, pointing to a place for me to stand. Then she sat at the piano and launched into the first song.

Right away, everybody started singing. We sang for the entire period. The class even went over by a couple of minutes so that we could finish one of the songs.

I guess music must have gotten my mind off my problems, because all of a sudden the day was practically over. I was surprised when the bell rang. Trying not to put much weight on my sore foot, I hurried back to homeroom for dismissal.

It was the end of my first day at Midway, and I was actually still alive. Of course, I hadn't made friends with any of the girls.

As for boys, forget it. My most meaningful contact with a boy took place when Mr. Barrazutti passed out the Midway basketball schedule. The boy who sat in front of me turned around and handed one to me. He said, "Here." And I said, "Thanks." Hot stuff, huh?

When the bell rang, everybody stood up and made a mad rush for the door. My blister felt as big as Mount Vesuvius. I couldn't wait to take off my shoes.

"So?" Kevin asked me, walking over to my locker while I got my jacket. "How'd it go?"

I didn't want to sound like I was feeling sorry for myself—even though I was. So i just said, "Okay."

Kevin was saying something about short-wave radios as he walked me down the corridor and out of the school. I didn't listen closely, though, because all I could think about was my foot. I thought it might be bleeding, but I didn't want anybody to see me check it.

My mother was parked right in front of the school, which was pretty embarrassing. But at least nobody knew who she was. I saw her searching for me through the hordes of students. "Look, Megan, there's your mother," Kevin said, a little too loudly, I thought.

He walked me over to the car and said hello to her, then ran off in the other direction to catch his bus.

Sliding into the car, a major feeling of relief came over me. At least I was someplace familiar. The first thing I did was ease off my shoe. My heel wasn't bleeding, but it was all red and raw.

"So? How'd it go?" My mother's usual perky voice sounded strained. I knew she didn't want to offend me by prying, but she just couldn't help herself.

Answering was easy, since I had already decided to keep my misery to myself. "Oh, pretty good," I said, trying to sound upbeat.

"Did you meet any interesting kids? Anybody you might want to be friends with?" she asked.

"Yup," I said. Whatever else you could say about Curtis and Ira, they were interesting. And there was that girl, Terri, too. I wanted to be friends with her.

Mom looked terribly relieved. "I knew it," she said.

We didn't say much more, and when I got home, I went straight to my room. "I've got a lot of homework," I told her, happy to be telling the truth for a change.

When I went to Mead, my routine had always been to handle my homework and then call Amanda. This time I couldn't wait. I had to call her right away.

"You can't imagine how horrible it is!" I wailed over the phone. "It's four million times worse than I thought it would be!"

"Are you sure?" she said in that mischievous voice of hers. "Maybe it's only four hundred times worse." I could just see the funny little grin on her face.

"Stop teasing," I told her. "My whole life is going down the tubes. I mean it."

Then, I told her everything. How I got lost,

about my Pilgrim father shoes and the blister, about how I'd met Terri and then those rude boys had come along. And worst of all, how I had made a total fool of myself in biology by running on and on about the make-up of cells!

"Relax, Megan," Amanda said. "There's nothing wrong with being smart."

"There is at Midway!" I insisted.

I could tell Amanda was stumped. "Hmm-mmm," she murmured, stalling. "Well, that girl, Terri, sounds nice."

"I know, but I don't have any classes with her, and I didn't even see her again all day," I complained. "That's how big Midway is."

"Well, what about that girl Rosemary in your bio class? Maybe you'll get to be friends with her."

"Fat chance," I said.

"Why not?" Amanda asked.

"Oh, I don't know. She's real popular."

"So what? You'll be real popular soon, too."

This conversation was getting frustrating. Amanda didn't seem to believe me about how awful Midway was! "I don't know how to make friends with anyone," I blurted out. My eyes were starting to sting.

"You made friends with *me*," Amanda said quietly. Her voice felt exactly like a hug.

"It was different with you!" I said. "We were

born to be best friends! This is all, I don't know, so artificial."

"Maybe it's just unfamiliar, Megan. Besides, life goes on. I mean, here we are, having our daily gab session, right?"

I had to laugh. "You're right. Enough of this doom and gloom. Tell me what's happening at Mead. Tell me everything."

"Okay. Are you ready for this?" Amanda giggled. "Miss Grey picked Trudy Puckett to be the lead in the spring semester play."

"Oh, no! Trudy's a terrible actress!"

She told me everything, all the little details I'd been so interested in before. But now, it seemed so—so foggy, like it was a million miles away. And Amanda seemed to go on and on about everything.

A wave of panic hit me. What was happening? Was our friendship already slipping away? I knew then that things would never be the same between us again.

CHAPTER

6

$\mathbb{S}$lowly, very slowly, I got to feel a little more comfortable at Midway. One thing that helped was that I started wearing more laid-back clothes—the kind I used to wear on weekends when I was at Mead.

"Isn't that outfit a little casual?" my mother asked one morning when I came down for breakfast wearing my gray sweatshirt and black jeans.

"No," I answered firmly. She raised her eyebrows and gave my dad a look. But they didn't say anything else about it.

Even the classes at Midway picked up. After a few weeks, we started learning new stuff. Pretty soon everyone else caught up to where

I was. So instead of being a giant "brain," I was just another smart kid. Except in biology, of course. There, they still thought of me as a science whiz.

On weekends, I started baby-sitting for a family who had moved into the house across the street. They had two little boys, Waylon and Peter Cooper, and they were really cute kids. Waylon was four and Peter was two.

Every dollar I earned, I stashed away. In the spring I planned to get some really awesome clothes.

After a month and a half at Midway, I still didn't have a single friend! I kind of liked the girl next to me in chorus. Her name was Merilee Evans. But I never really got a chance to talk to her, because Mrs. Friedman always kept us overtime. We had to run to homeroom the minute chorus was over.

A few times, I ran into Terri in the cafeteria. That was always great.

"Hey, Megan!" she'd call out whenever she saw me. Her grin reminded me of Amanda. "How's it going?"

We ate lunch together a few times, but usually, as soon as we'd start talking, someone would come over and pull her away. She told me she was a peer counselor, who helped kids talk about some of their problems. This made me feel better, because I was beginning to think she liked everyone else more than she liked me.

Maybe I was too depressed to make friends. I don't know. Anyhow, I didn't make any. When my father said we were going over to the MacArthurs' for dinner in the middle of February, I was happy for the first time in a month.

Now, it's true Kevin and I saw each other every day in homeroom, but we hadn't really talked since New Year's Eve. I kept insisting everything was fine when he asked how things were going. That sort of ended any real conversation we might have had.

But that night at his house, all my troubles came pouring out over a game of chess.

"Megan, you're not concentrating," he said as he took my queen. "That's two games in a row you've blown completely. What's wrong?"

I finally blurted out the truth. "What's wrong is, I don't have any friends at Midway!"

He pressed his lips together and thought. "What about the kids in your classes? Don't you talk to them?"

"I'm talking about *friends*, Kevin," I said. "Not classmates."

"Well, um, what about me?" he asked, pushing up his glasses on his nose. They were now taped together in three different places.

I shrugged. "I know we're friends, but that's

different," I said, trying to find the right way to put it without hurting his feelings.

Kevin seemed to understand immediately. "I know. I'm a boy."

I flipped over my king on the chessboard. "I resign. I don't feel like playing anyway."

Kevin put his hands on his knees and looked over at me. "You need cheering up, and I've got just the thing," he said. He opened the door and led the way to the attic stairs. "Follow me—whooo, hahaha!" he said in a Dracula voice, rubbing his hands together.

In the attic was this incredible setup with dials, lights, buttons, a microphone, and headphones. "What is it?" I asked, checking it out.

"It's a shortwave radio!" he said excitedly. He sat down in front of it and pulled up a chair for me to sit next to him. "Wait till you hear—I've already picked up North Dakota and Kansas!"

"You mean you can hear people talking that far away?"

Kevin nodded. "Not only that, they can hear me! Talk about making friends, Megan—you should get one of these!"

I couldn't help laughing. "Maybe you're right," I said, slipping on the pair of headphones he gave me.

Pretty soon, we were talking with a guy

named Harvey, in Duluth, Minnesota. Harvey was a farmer, and he'd been doing this for years. He said if you got a special type of antenna you could extend your range and talk to people all over the world. Boy, did that get Kevin excited—until he found out it cost over a hundred dollars.

I was pretty excited, too. Just imagine, having friends you talked to every day, but had never met in person. It would be kind of like having a pen pal, but over the radio.

By the time we came back downstairs, it was time to go. I was feeling a whole lot better. In fact, I had the strong impression that somehow, my life was going to change from that moment on.

I didn't know how right I was.

The next day was Monday. The weather was sunny, and actually kind of warm. I guess you'd call it a February thaw. I walked to school that day feeling kind of "up." At least I knew I had one friend—Kevin. And I suppose I was getting used to Midway, too.

When I got to homeroom, there was Kevin, smiling and joking around. Mr. Barrazutti was extra funny, too. By the time I got to biology, I actually had a smile on my face.

I sat down and opened my book, when a

voice next to me said, "Hi, Megan!" I turned around to see who it was, and I nearly went into shock. There, sitting next to me, giving me a great big smile, was Rosemary Weil!

"Guess what, Megan?" she said, touching me on the arm. "I got Amy Johnson to switch places with me so we could sit next to each other. Isn't that great?"

Well, I was just speechless. I couldn't believe that Rosemary Weil had gone to the trouble of switching seats so she could sit next to me!

Ms. Cornwall was standing in the doorway, talking to somebody in the hall. "I had to promise Amy an invite to my next party. But it was worth it," Rosemary said, winking at me. "I hope *you* can come, too."

My mouth opened, and I said something brilliant like, "Well, um, ah, you, ah, well, uh . . ."

"Great!" said Rosemary, beaming at me. "I've been wanting to invite you over ever since you first came here, but I've been so busy with cheerleading and everything. You know how it is."

"Oh, sure," I lied.

"Oh, and we're all going shopping at the mall on Saturday. Can you come? My mom can pick you up in our minivan, okay?"

I blinked about sixteen times, just trying to

see straight, I was so thrilled and surprised. "Um, okay, I guess," I mumbled. I was trying desperately to be cool.

"Fabu! Utterly excellent!" Rosemary squealed. Leaning over her shoulder, she called out, "Farrah! Megan can come shopping with us. Isn't that fabu?"

"Excellent!" Farrah squealed back.

I bit my lip as Ms. Cornwall came in and started the lesson. I was staring at the words in my textbook, but they kept dancing around, forming the word "YAHOO!!!"

It looked like the big freeze was finally over. I had found a friend at last—or rather, she had found me.

And what a friend—only the most popular girl at Midway Junior High!

CHAPTER

7

By the end of the day, Rosemary's other friends were already starting to look at me differently. A couple of them even said hello to me between classes.

When I left the building, I heard someone call out, "Bye, Megan! See you tomorrow!" I whipped my head around. It was Rosemary. She was waving and smiling at me. I waved back, and started walking home with a definite bounce in my step.

That night at dinner, I looked up from my plate of ravioli. "Mom," I said, "you are really an excellent cook."

My mother looked absolutely stunned, and so did my dad. "Well, isn't that nice," she said, acting surprised. "I got a compliment—for serving frozen food!"

"Amazing," my dad said.

"Come on, don't act so shocked," I said. "You know I think you're both the greatest."

My mother choked on her tomato sauce and started wiping her lips with a napkin. But from the look in her eyes, I could tell she was happy.

"Now, you're *sure* you're all right, Meggie?" my dad said, still joking around.

"Never better!" I said.

"By the way, honey," my mother told me. "Amanda called."

"Great!" I said. I hadn't talked to her in ages. I guess I'd been feeling too down to call her very often. "May I please be excused from the table?" My parents nodded, and I bounded up to my room, two stairs at a time.

I tried calling Amanda to tell her the good news, but her line was busy for a long time. I made a mental note to try her again tomorrow.

The next day in biology, Rosemary was sitting next to me again. She gave me a bright smile and leaned over toward me. "I wanted to call you last night, but I forgot to get your phone number," she said, just as Ms. Cornwall walked to the board to begin her lecture.

My heart did a flip-flop. Rosemary Weil wanted to call me!

During the class, when Ms. Cornwall turned to the board to draw some genetic charts, Rosemary leaned toward me again. "Psst!" she signaled, holding out a stick of gum. I took it, and put it in my pocket. We weren't allowed to chew gum during classes.

"Thanks," I breathed.

"What's your next class?" she asked.

"English," I told her.

"I'll walk you," she said.

"Okay," I said. What a conversationalist, huh?

After class, Rosemary started walking down the hall with me. Heather Lockwood was walking up the hall in our direction. She gave Rosemary a startled look.

"Hey, Roe," Heather said. "Aren't you going to gym?"

Instead of answering right away, Rosemary turned to me. "My best friends all call me Roe. You can, too, if you want." Then she turned back to Heather. "Yes, I am. I was just walking Megan to English. Want to come?"

"Sure," Heather said, giving me a curious look. I tried to look cool, but I did feel awkward walking next to Heather. She'd been sitting next to me in social studies for weeks, and she'd never even said hello.

"Did you see that new lipstick that comes with its own brush?" Rosemary asked me suddenly.

I shook my head. Suddenly my lips felt horribly naked.

"It's really neat," she said, pulling a small flat container out of her purse. "The brush goes right in here. Using a lip brush is the best way to put on lipstick."

"Really?" I blurted out. I didn't mean to sound so uncool. It just sort of happened.

Heather looked bored and a little amused at the same time. "Roe, we're going to be late," she complained.

Rosemary turned to me and said, "Meet me in the cafeteria, okay? We'll have lunch together."

"Okay," I said.

She and Heather turned around and left in a hurry. Then Rosemary turned back to me suddenly. "Oh, Megan, don't forget to save me a seat," she called out. "Okay?"

I almost fainted dead away from happiness.

Once Rosemary Weil was my friend, it was as if someone had opened a magic door.

People who had never paid the least attention to me were staring at me, and saying hello. All of a sudden, everyone wanted to know who Megan Murray was!

By the end of the week, I was actually starting to feel like a part of Rosemary's gang. If Rosemary was the unofficial queen of Midway

Junior High, then I had risen from lowly serf to favored lady-in-waiting.

On Saturday, we were all going shopping together at the mall: Roe, Heather, Farrah—and *I*!

I was really looking forward to it. I'd earned enough money baby-sitting so I could get some really cool clothes. I was sure that if I learned to dress like Rosemary and her friends, I would be super comfortable with them.

Not that being comfortable mattered. What mattered, of course, was being popular. I sure was ready for that.

Friday night I finally thought to call Amanda. I'd been so busy all week it had slipped my mind entirely.

"Guess what?" I told her, filling her in on everything. "I've finally made a friend! She'll never replace you of course, but it's so great. Oh, Amanda, I'm soooo happy!"

"Megan, that's super! I won't say I told you so . . . yes, I will. I told you so."

"You told me so," I admitted. "Maybe you should become a gypsy fortune teller."

"I already am," Amanda insisted.

"Okay, so tell my fortune," I said. "What's next for our heroine?"

"Ah," Amanda said mysteriously, "for that, you will have to wait until tomorrow. I see in my crystal ball that your friend Amanda is finally free to get together."

"Great!" I shouted. Then, "Oh, no, I just remembered—Rosemary asked me to go shopping with her and a bunch of girls at the mall tomorrow."

I could hear the catch in Amanda's voice. "Oh . . . that's okay, Megan. We can do it next week—"

"No, of course not," I said, a little too quickly. "I'll tell Rosemary I can't go."

"No, you will not!" Amanda insisted. "You've finally got yourself a new friend, and you've got to get to know her. It's important for you. I'll always be here, Megan. I'm not going anywhere, you know that."

"Thanks, Amanda. You're the best," I said. "I will go with them, then—if you're sure you wouldn't be hurt."

"Don't be ridiculous," she said. "Have a great time. And, Megan, be yourself, okay? You're great just the way you are."

After I hung up, I thought about that one. "Just the way you are." Who was I, anyway? I didn't have a clue. I almost called Amanda right back to ask her, but then I thought that would be too embarrassing.

So I didn't call. What a colossal mistake.

CHAPTER

The next morning I got ready for my shopping trip with Roe and her other friends. I had all my baby-sitting money with me—fifty-eight dollars. I figured that was enough to buy something really super.

"You're wearing lipstick?" my mother said when I came downstairs to wait for Roe. She seemed surprised, and not at all happy about it.

"Yes," I said, as definitely as I could manage. "All the girls at Midway wear lipstick."

I could tell she didn't have the heart to argue with me about it. Instead, she let out a sigh. "Oh, well," she said. "When in Rome, I suppose."

Just then, Roe's van pulled up to the house.

"I've got to go," I told my mother, giving her a quick kiss.

The van was packed with Rosemary's crowd: Farrah, Heather, and of course, Roe herself. We laughed and joked all the way there. Rosemary did a terrific imitation of Ms. Cornwall. I couldn't help laughing at it.

"First, we go to Shazam," Rosemary said when we got to the mall. "Megan, I know exactly what you need."

All the girls giggled. For a second, it made me uncomfortable. It sounded exactly like the giggles I'd heard the first day of school, and every day after that for weeks. Then I decided they were just having fun, so I put it out of my mind.

In Shazam, all of us went nuts trying things on. I put on some spring stuff, and modeled some jumpsuits. Then Rosemary walked up to me with this really fancy outfit and said, "Try this on, Megan—it's *you*."

I looked at it. It was cute, I guess, but I would never have described it as "me." The dress had a short midriff top and a flared miniskirt. That might have been okay, except that the material was bright yellow with red polka dots. Kind of loud, I thought.

"I was sort of looking for school stuff," I said.

"No, no, no. This is for the *party*!" Rosemary told me. "It's a dress-up party."

"What party?"

"*My* party! You know, it's at my house, tonight."

I bit my lip. She had said she'd be having a party soon, but that was on Monday, and she hadn't said when. "Oh, yeah, I know about it," I lied.

"You're coming, aren't you?" Rosemary looked at me with pleading eyes. "It won't be the same without you."

The other girls giggled again. I hadn't even asked my parents' permission to go out that night. What if they said no?

"Of course I'm coming!" I said. "I wouldn't miss it for anything."

"Fabu!" Rosemary cooed. "You'd better go try the dress on then."

In the fitting room, I looked at myself in the dress. I didn't think I looked too good in it. Not only that, it was so sexy, it was embarrassing. But everyone else oohhed and ahhed when I came out. I figured they knew better than I did what looked good. I was about to buy the outfit, when I looked at the price tag. It cost $89.99!

"Um, I think I'd like to shop around a little more before I buy anything," I mumbled.

"Why? Don't you love it?" Rosemary asked, looking almost hurt.

"Oh, I do," I lied. "But it's kind of expensive for me." I ran back into the fitting room before anyone could argue with me. A wave of relief passed over me.

"Come on," Rosemary said when I came out of the dressing room. "I know another neat place."

We all trooped after her to the lower level, to a store called Spangles. There, the clothes were a lot cheaper.

I saw Heather roll her eyes as she fingered a sweater. "Yuck," she said. "Acrylic."

But Rosemary didn't even hear her. She was pushing through a rack of dresses with a look of concentration on her face. Then all of a sudden, she started shrieking, "Megan! Megan! Come over here! Look at this!"

I rushed over to where she was pulling a dress off the rack. It was an exact copy of the one I'd just tried on at Shazam!

"They have it in your size, too!" she said triumphantly. "And it's only $39.99! Now you've got no excuse!"

There wasn't much I could do at that point. Swallowing my doubts, I put down my forty hard-earned dollars and bought the dress.

"Oh, you're going to look so cool," Rosemary said. "Isn't she, Heather?"

"Oh, so cool," Heather said in a voice that sounded just the tiniest bit mean.

"Don't worry about Heather," Rosemary whispered as the clerk wrapped up my new dress. "She's just jealous of you."

"She is?" I said, feeling a little confused. I didn't always understand the way Rosemary and her friends acted with each other. But I promised myself that no matter what, I'd learn. After all, the thing I wanted more than anything else was to be *just like them*.

I had no trouble getting permission from my parents to go to Rosemary's party. I think they were thrilled I'd been invited *anywhere*.

After dinner, Mom drove me over to Roe's house. I had put my coat on in my bedroom so Mom wouldn't see my new dress. I knew she wouldn't be too thrilled with it. I was kind of nervous, so I didn't talk much on the way there. I waved good-bye to my mom the minute Rosemary opened the door. She waved back and drove away.

"Hi, Megan," Rosemary said.

I looked at her in total shock. She was wearing jeans and a shirt with sequins.

"I thought you said this was a dress-up party," I said, taking off my coat.

"Oh, it is," Rosemary said, airily. "I was going to wear my party dress, but it had a big spot on it. That's why I had to wear this." She touched the sequins on her shirt and flashed me a smile. "But don't worry—you look great."

"Thanks," I said. I felt totally foolish standing there in my skimpy new party dress. I was unbelievably cold, too.

Just then Jason Wright, the captain of the Midway football team, walked up to Rosemary and put an arm around her. Jason had been Rosemary's boyfriend since the beginning of the school year. "This has to be Megan," he said.

"Megan, you know Jason Wright, don't you?" Rosemary asked.

"Yes, hi," I said. Everyone at Midway knew who Jason Wright was. But Kevin always called him Jason Wrong. Kevin told me that last year Jason had stuffed him into a locker. With his All-American looks, it was hard to believe Jason could do something like that, but I guess you can never tell.

"Hey, Megan," Jason said, giving me a small smile before he turned to Rosemary. "Where are the other sodas, Roe? We can't find them."

"You go in, Megan," Rosemary said sweetly. "I want to help Jason put out some more drinks."

She pointed into the living room, where a bunch of kids were standing around listening to music. No one was dressed up.

Trying not to look nervous, I walked in. Everybody in the room turned to look at me. Then they all looked away. My face turned as red as the dots on my dress.

Farrah was standing by the snacks, stuffing a bunch of pretzels into her mouth. She gave me a little wave, so I walked over to her.

"Rosemary told me this was a dress-up party," I said.

"Really?" Farrah replied coolly. "She didn't tell *me* that."

"Now I feel like a real jerk," I said.

Farrah just shrugged and walked away. That made me feel more foolish than ever. But I pretended that I didn't care. I took a plate and loaded it with a bunch of potato chips.

In fact, I spent a lot of time at the food table, plundering the munchies, while everyone else flirted and danced.

One boy and girl I didn't know were on the couch. First, they were just talking. Then, they started gazing into each other's eyes. Soon after that, they began kissing like crazy. Where in the world were Rosemary's parents, anyway?

I felt really dumb standing there all by myself, trying to look like I was having a good time. Fortunately, Rosemary's Lhasa Apso walked into the room just then. He looked everybody over and then approached me.

"Hey, Butler," I said, kneeling down to pat the little dog's head. "How you doing, boy?" He put his furry chin on my knee. "Well, at least someone appreciates my company," I told him.

"Okay, everybody, game time!" Rosemary announced after a while. She walked over to the stereo and shut off the music. "We're going to play Seven Minutes in Heaven."

I wasn't sure what she was talking about, but I found out soon enough.

"For those of you who haven't played before, here's what we do," Roe said, rubbing her hands together excitedly. "Each girl picks a boy's name from the hat. Then that couple has to go into the other room—alone—for seven minutes."

Farrah handed Rosemary a straw hat filled with little pieces of paper. "Let's see—who should go first?" She looked us all over with a mischievous gleam in her eyes. Then she giggled and stuck the hat in front of me. "You're on, Megan!"

I put my hand in, and pulled out a paper with the name "Vance Lockwood" on it. Reading over my shoulder, Rosemary announced the name loudly. A tall, red-haired boy with freckles stepped out of a group of boys. He looked pretty uncomfortable.

Rosemary pointed to a door off the living

room. "Good luck, Vance," she said with a little snicker. "And don't worry about the time. We'll watch the clock out here. Ready, set, go!"

Vance and I walked into the next room, and closed the door. The room looked like a den, but the lights were all out, except for a candle, so it was hard to tell.

"Now what?" I asked.

Vance looked pretty embarrassed. "Oh, we just have to make noise and stuff," he explained.

"Like what?" I asked.

"Like . . ." and he let out a half moan, half shout. "Oh, Megan!" He said it loud enough for the whole neighborhood to hear.

I nearly died.

"Now you say, 'Oh, Vance,' " he told me.

"No way," I said. "This is stupid."

"I know," he said. "But the guys will laugh at me if they think I didn't get a kiss."

"Oh, okay," I said. "Oh, Vance." I didn't say it very loudly.

Vance looked worried. "We better say something else, like hmmmmm."

The two of us stood there, letting out these odd sounds every so often. Our "seven minutes" felt more like an eternity. I couldn't wait for them to be over.

"Um, would you mind kissing me so I can get some lipstick on my face?" Vance asked when our time was almost up. "Otherwise, the guys will rank on me."

I could understand him not wanting to be teased, so I said, "Oh, all right," and gave him a quick peck on the side of his face. He walked over to the candle and bent down.

"Can you see it?" he asked.

"Yes," I told him.

"Great. Thanks," he said.

Finally, Rosemary announced, "Time's up, you two!" Everybody cheered and stamped their feet as we came out. The guys all congratulated Vance, and the girls looked at me and giggled their heads off.

When the next couple went in, Vance gave me a smile and a wink. I looked away. My cheeks were burning with embarrassment.

Fortunately, it was already eleven o'clock. "My mother's going to be here any minute," I said, walking over to the closet and finding my coat. I said a quick good-bye to Rosemary and stepped outside. The fake smile on my face disappeared the second the cold air hit me in the face. By the time my mother showed up, I was freezing. I ran to the car and got in.

"Hi, Sweetie," she said. "Hey, you're shivering!"

"It's pretty cold out," I said.

"Did you have a good time?"

"Pretty good," I said, putting my hands in front of the heater.

My mother looked confused. "Why were you standing outside?"

I gritted my teeth. "I don't want to talk about it," I said.

The next morning, I stayed in bed late, thinking about the night before. I was definitely not ready for boy-girl parties. Not that kind, anyway. But I still wanted to be Rosemary's friend.

So you can imagine how relieved I was when she called. "I'm sorry I was such a dud last night," I said.

"You were not!" Rosemary said. "You were fine. I mean, you did look a *little* uncomfortable."

"I was," I admitted, hoping she'd still like me. "I never—I mean, I'm just not that comfortable with guys yet."

"I understand," Rosemary said. "Lots of girls aren't. Anyway, I called to ask you for a teeny tiny favor," she said in a little-girl voice.

"Sure, anything!" I said. I was really happy to be able to do something for Rosemary. She'd been so good to me, and I felt like I hadn't done one thing for her.

"Great," she said. "Well, see, I've been having a little problem with my biology homework, and I was wondering, did you finish it yet? Because you're so great in biology, and I'm such a dummy at it . . ."

"You are not!" I said.

"Well, could I ask you a few questions?" she begged. "Please, please, pleeeease?"

I laughed. "Of course," I said. "Shoot."

She shot. And shot and shot and shot. By the time we got through, I'd given her almost the whole assignment, wrapped up with a ribbon.

"Gee, thanks, Megan. You're a genius, and a real friend."

I had never given answers to anyone before. In fact, I had been doing a lot of stuff lately I'd never done before.

But I hadn't forgotten what it was like before Rosemary became my friend. Anything was better than that, I told myself.

Even if it meant changing who I was.

CHAPTER

9

ow that I was friends with Rosemary Weil, the days seemed to fly. By the time March rolled around, I was basically settled in at Midway.

Every morning, I'd walk into homeroom and talk to Kevin. He would fill me in on his latest adventures. Usually he'd be excited about some new software program he had discovered, or a chess game he'd won. But what really made his eyes shine was his shortwave radio.

"Megan!" he cried one day when I sat down with him by the window. "You won't believe it— I got Mexico City last night! I was talking to a kid whose parents work at the Embassy there."

"Fantastic," I said.

"We were speaking in Spanish, too. He said he would help me learn."

"Wow, that's really neat, Kev," I said. "I wish I had someone to practice French with."

"Aha! I already thought of that!" Kevin said with a grin. "This weekend, I'm going to try to reach Haiti, so you'll have someone to speak French with!"

"Great," I said, right before the bell rang. Kevin didn't walk me to biology anymore. Ever since I'd made friends with Rosemary, she'd meet me outside homeroom and we'd walk to class together.

I knew that Rosemary wasn't exactly Kevin's favorite person. But the nasty girl he had first described to me was nothing like the sweet one who had befriended me. Also, once Kevin knew that Rosemary and I were friends, he never said a mean word about her.

That day, Rosemary came up the hall to meet me with a disturbed look on her face.

"What's the matter, Roe?" I asked right away.

Instead of answering, she made a face. Then she pulled me into the girls' room at the end of the hall. "I tried calling you last night. Where were you?" she complained.

"At my grandmother's," I told her. I was worried that something was really wrong.

"Well, you've got to help me with our biology

assignment," she said frantically. She took out a pencil. "I read it over and over, and I was totally lost!"

I glanced at my watch. We had exactly four minutes until class. "Okay," I said. "What do you want to know?"

"Well, for starters, what's cell specialization?" She said it like she was speaking a foreign language.

"Um, it just means that different kinds of cells have different jobs to do."

"Oh. Okay. I understand." She didn't look like she understood one bit. "Look, I don't have time to go over it all. Could you just tell me the answers?"

I hesitated. But the look on her face made it clear she was about to get really mad. So I opened up my notebook and did what she said. "Don't tell Ms. Cornwall, okay?" I mumbled, ashamed.

"What do you think I am, an idiot?" she snapped. But as soon as she'd filled in her homework sheet, she gave me a big smile and walked toward the mirror. "Thanks, Megan. You're really an angel," she said, quickly running a brush through her hair.

More like a cheater, I thought. But I shoved that notion way back into my brain. There wasn't any law against helping a friend, was there?

"By the way," Rosemary asked, "did Farrah mention the party she's having this Saturday?"

"No," I said.

"It doesn't matter," Rosemary said with a shrug of her shoulders. "If I say so, you're invited."

"I can't go anyway. I'm busy on Saturday." When it came to parties, I was always busy. Being friends with Rosemary was great, but going to parties with her and the gang was total agony.

Rosemary threw me a mysterious grin. "Oh? Do you have a date or something?" she asked.

"No!" I said, blushing like crazy.

"You do!" Rosemary said excitedly. "I can tell!"

"I'm baby-sitting for a couple of little boys!" I insisted.

"Oh, sure, sure," she said with a giggle, as if she didn't believe it. "*Little boys*, huh? Hey! Why don't you bring them to the party?"

My cheeks were burning. "They're pre-schoolers, Rosemary," I said, holding the door open for her.

"Oh, Megan," Rosemary said with a sigh. "You're impossible. Why would you want to baby-sit on a Saturday night? That's so dumb."

"So I can make money," I told her.

"Yes, but when you shop you never buy anything. All you ever got was that one party dress. I'm beginning to think you're really cheap!"

She said it with a laugh, but I still felt embarrassed. Next Saturday, I decided, I would spend all my baby-sitting money on something really cool. Something that would make me look good enough to be Rosemary Weil's best friend.

The next Saturday, while Rosemary's mother tooted the van's horn, I stuffed my money in my wallet. "Almost a hundred dollars," I murmured to myself. "That should be enough to buy something fabu."

"Want to try Warfield's?" I suggested when we got to the mall. "I need a new sweater like crazy." That was the way Heather and Farrah talked, so I was talking like that, too.

Rosemary wrinkled her nose. "Megan," she said, making a face. "I can't believe you. Warfield's is so tacky. Let's go to Shazam."

I bit my lip. Why did their favorite boutique have to be the most expensive one in the whole mall?

"Shazam? Okay," I said, with a cool shrug.

"You need something radical," Rosemary told me.

The minute we walked into the store, Rosemary started squealing. "Ooh! Look at *those*!"

On a table were a bunch of fuzzy angora sweaters, decorated with patches of leather, buttons, shells, and feathers.

Rosemary headed straight for them. She picked up a shocking pink sweater and handed it to me. "Oh, Megan, this is intensely you!" she cried.

"I think it's kind of loud . . ." I began. But I shut up when Rosemary shot me a disappointed look.

"Why do I even bother to go shopping with you?" she asked bitterly. "It's a total waste of time!"

"Hold it up in front of you," Farrah suggested.

I did. The color made my skin look like a neon sign.

"Fabu! You've got to try it on," Rosemary begged.

"And look," Heather added, picking out a pair of mustard slacks from a nearby rack. "These go with it perfectly!"

"The colors are a little strange together, aren't they?" I asked.

"No, they're awesome," Rosemary insisted.

Before I knew it, I was in the dressing room, wearing the sweater and slacks.

I thought I looked like a circus clown, but Rosemary and Farrah wouldn't stop gushing over the outfit.

"You look fantastic!" Rosemary told me, over and over. "You've got to buy them."

"I don't know about the fit," I said in a tiny voice. The sweater went off one shoulder, which was really strange. Weren't sweaters supposed to keep a person warm?

"It's so much better than those other dorky clothes you wear," Rosemary said.

My cheeks got red. And of course, I bought the outfit. I never wanted them to call me dorky again, that was for sure.

Rosemary, Farrah, and Heather went off searching through other racks of clothing while I stood in line at the cashier's counter. I could hear them giggling their heads off.

Then I heard a friendly voice behind me. "Hi, Megan!" it said.

I turned around and found myself looking into Terri's smiling dark eyes. "I haven't seen you in ages! How's it going?"

"Terri! Hi!" This time the smile that came to my face was genuine.

"Did you buy something?" Terri asked.

"A sweater and slacks," I told her, hoping she wouldn't ask to look in the bag the sales-clerk handed me. "Are you getting something?"

"Oh, no. I'm just returning something for my stepmom," Terri said in a quiet voice. "I don't shop in here. It's a little expensive for me. But I'm glad I ran into you." With a smile, she pulled an envelope from her pocket. It was addressed to me!

"I got your address from Mrs. Cook in the principal's office," she said with a grin. I ripped open the envelope. Inside was an invitation to an ice skating party.

"I always like to invite at least one new friend to my birthday parties. It's kind of a tradition with me," she explained. "Do you think you can come?"

"Well, I'm not a very good ice skater," I warned her.

But Terri just laughed. "Oh, that doesn't matter," she said, with a grin. "It's just for fun. There won't be any boys there either, so none of us have to worry if we look dumb."

I had to giggle at that.

"I may have to change the time to noon, though, because the rink may be rented before that. I can let you know at school, or if I don't see you, I'll tell Merilee Evans. She sits next to you in chorus, right?"

"Right."

"She lives down my block. She and I—" Terri looked like she was going to say more, but then she got a funny, frozen look on her face.

I turned around and there were Rosemary, Heather, and Farrah, staring at Terri and me.

"We're leaving, Megan," Rosemary said, her eyes fixed on Terri in an icy stare.

"Right away," Farrah added.

"Are you coming?" Rosemary prompted me.

"Okay," I said, puzzled.

Terri seemed to avoid their eyes. "I'll catch you another time, Megan," she said.

Rosemary took my arm and pulled me out of the store. She grabbed so hard my shoulder hurt.

"What was that all about?" I blurted out when we got to the main promenade.

"I can't believe who you were talking to," Rosemary said with a pout.

"What do you mean?" I asked, worried.

"Don't you know what Terri did to Roe?" Farrah said, looking at me like I was from another planet. "She beat her out for cheerleading captain!"

Rosemary turned to Farrah and snapped, "Everybody knows I'm better than her, but she influenced the judges."

"Huh?" I said, looking from one angry girl to another.

"She got the judges to consider grades when they picked the captain," Rosemary said tightly.

"I don't know if she's the one who did that, Roe," Farrah said quietly. "My mom said the PTA was pushing for—"

"I don't care," Rosemary interrupted. "As far as I'm concerned, Terri Lawson is a complete zero."

For one uncomfortable moment, the four of us stood there, not saying anything.

"Why was she talking to *you*, anyway?" Farrah asked, looking over at me.

I gulped. "She, uh, she invited me to a party."

"Well, you're not going, are you?" The glare Rosemary was giving me was so heated it could have launched a spaceship.

"Of course not!" I said as forcefully as I could.

That seemed to break the tension. "Good," Rosemary purred. "Ugh, she makes me so— come on, let's go to the Food Court. I don't even want to be on the same level with that creep."

It was crystal clear to me that if I wanted to be Rosemary's friend, I had better steer clear of Terri. I looked down at the tops of my sneakers as we walked along. Why did it have to be like this? Why did I have to make an enemy to keep a friend?

Right before Spring Break, I told Merilee to tell Terri I couldn't go to her party.

"Oh, no," Merilee said, a disappointed look in her eyes. "Why not?"

I made some dumb excuse about my parents taking me to visit relatives, and Merilee seemed to believe me. But when we started singing, my voice was awfully weak.

I thought that was the end of everything until a couple of days later. I was in my room working on an English assignment when the phone rang.

"Megan?" a girl whose voice sounded familiar said. "It's Terri."

I was glad she couldn't see my beet-red face over the phone. "Terri? Hi."

For a minute I didn't know what to do. I knew Rosemary wouldn't like me talking to her. On the other hand, Rosemary wasn't around. "I'm sorry I wasn't at your party," I said. "I bet it was fun."

"It was," she said. "But don't feel too bad about missing it, because guess what? I'm having another one! That's what I'm calling about."

"You're kidding?"

"Not another ice skating party, just a regular boy-girl party. But you don't have to bring a date or anything like that. I'm just having a bunch of kids from school—"

It killed me to say no, but I had to. "I—I, um, I can't make that one either," I said. Whispered, really. I was so embarrassed and upset.

"Gee," she said. "Don't you even want to know when it is?"

My breath caught in my throat. She'd

caught me! "Um, it's just that I'm really busy right now, and, um, my mom has been sick, and—" I felt lower than a worm.

"Oh, okay," Terri said slowly. From the sound of her voice, I don't think she really believed me. "Sorry to hear about your mom. Well, see you around, then." She hung up, and I just sat there, feeling like a real jerk.

I could tell I'd hurt her feelings, and that was the last thing I wanted to do. Terri was so nice, and I really did want to be her friend. I had messed it up royally now. She'd never invite me anywhere again, that was for sure.

So Spring Break came and went, and instead of going to parties and having fun, I just hid from everyone. I didn't even go shopping with Rosemary and Farrah when they asked me. My new pink sweater cured me of doing that again.

Amanda called a couple times, but whenever I got the message I put off calling her back. I knew she would never understand everything I was going through at Midway.

The last night of vacation, I saw Kevin MacArthur. His family came over for dinner, and afterward, we went for a walk. I hadn't really talked much to Kevin for a while, other than seeing him in homeroom. I guess I was too busy socializing with my other friends to pay much attention to him.

That's why it startled me when I looked at him that night. There was something different about him . . .

"Kevin, you got new glasses!" I said when it hit me. "Wow, they look fantastic!" They really did, too. They were photo-graded, and the frames were this cool red wire. Best of all, they didn't have any tape on them!

Something else was different about Kevin, too. "Have you grown or something?" I asked, looking him over.

"You noticed!" he crowed, slapping his hands together. "Two inches since January."

"That's incredible," I said, shaking my head in amazement. That really was a lot. In fact, you couldn't really call Kevin short anymore.

"Maybe kids will stop teasing me now," he said.

"Oh, come on," I said. "Who teases you about your height?"

Kevin made a face. "Try Jason Wright, Rosemary Weil, and their merry band—except for you, of course."

"Rosemary's not really that bad, once you get to know her," I said.

Kevin stopped and turned to face me. "She isn't?"

I was thrown off balance by his question. It took me a minute to reassure myself and say, "Of course not. She's been really great to me."

"Well," he murmured thoughtfully, "I'm sure you know what you're doing."

"Hey," I said, "did you ever contact anybody in Haiti on your shortwave?"

Kevin shook his head. "I've run into some technical difficulties. My antenna isn't really that great. But I'm still trying."

"Can I come over the next time you do?"

That seemed to perk him up. "Great! Let's get together this weekend," he said, flashing an enormous smile. Then this crazy thought came to me.

Maybe I could invite Kevin to one of Rosemary's parties—as my date! I mean, nothing romantic or anything; just to have someone to be there with. Of course, first I'd have to lay the groundwork. I would point out casually to Rosemary and the others that Kevin was looking better, and taller. Of course, with Jason there, Kevin might not even agree to show up . . .

Just then, we noticed a jogger coming up to us. It was Rosemary! She nearly ran smack into us. "Megan!" she said, looking at me and then at Kevin. "Oh . . . I, uh—bye!"

With that, she ran off, covering her mouth like she was stifling a big laugh.

What in the world had gotten into her, I wondered. Soon enough, I found out.

CHAPTER 10

The next day, the strangest thing happened. Rosemary didn't meet me in the hall after homeroom. For a while, I wondered whether she was absent for the day. But when I got to biology, she was already sitting in her seat.

"I have to talk to you," she said through gritted teeth. I got the definite impression that she wasn't very happy about something.

"What's wrong?" I whispered. Ms. Cornwall had just walked to the board to start her lecture.

"I'll tell you at lunch," Roe answered in a clipped tone. Then she turned away and pretended not to be aware of me during the whole

97

class. Afterward, she hurried away before I could ask her anything else.

All morning, I worried about what could be making her so unfriendly. When I saw her at lunch, I knew it had to be something big.

Rosemary, Heather, and Farrah were seated together. Their unsmiling eyes were all glued on me as I made my way over to the table, tray in hand. Boy, did they look mad.

I took a deep breath and tried to sound casual. "Hi," I said. I think it came out a little shaky. "What's wrong? You look like you touched an electric wire or something."

"Sit down, Megan," Rosemary said to me, in a quiet but deadly tone of voice. Her dark eyes were aimed straight into mine. "We have to talk."

A bolt of fear shot through me. "Why?" I said. "What's going on?"

Rosemary gritted her teeth and took a deep breath. "Are you dating Kevin MacArthur?" she blurted out. "You'd better tell me the truth."

It was such a strange question that I didn't know what to say. Was I dating Kevin? I had never been on a date in my whole life! "No," I told her. "He's just a friend."

"You looked like more than friends when I saw you yesterday, Megan," she said accusingly. "And you go to his house sometimes, too, don't you?"

"Well, I've known Kevin since we were little kids," I said. "Besides, who cares?"

"I do!" Rosemary said. "When I saw you two, I nearly died of embarrassment. I mean, everybody knows that you're my friend, and that's fine. But if they see you with Kevin MacArthur, well—"

Rosemary put her hands on her head and leaned forward. She looked as if she were trying hard to find a way to break some terrible news to me. "Okay, Megan," she said finally. "It's like this: Kevin MacArthur is a first class, triple-A nerd. Now, I promise I won't tell anyone I saw you with him—"

Looking over at the other girls, I could tell it was already too late for that. Rosemary had obviously filled them in on everything.

"—*if* you promise to stop seeing him from now on. Even as a friend."

Needless to say, I was stunned. Kevin had been my friend when nobody else at school even cared who I was. He hadn't dropped me when I'd made friends with his worst enemies, either. I couldn't just abandon him now, could I?

Well, I'm sorry to say it—but that's exactly what I did. Even though I knew it was rotten,

I was just too terrified of losing Rosemary's friendship not to do what she said. Being a part of Midway's innest in-crowd had become too important to me.

The next day, I stayed out of homeroom as long as I could. When I went in, I gave Kevin a little wave instead of saying hello. Then, I opened my French book and pretended I had to study.

"I got Puerto Rico," he said, after the bell rang and we stood up to go to class.

Instead of saying, "Great," I just nodded and hurried off to the corridor.

The next day, Kevin met me at the door. "When you come over this weekend, do you want me to—" He was probably going to ask if I wanted him to rent a movie to watch after we'd finished with the shortwave.

But I didn't let him finish. "Listen, Kevin," I mumbled. "I really can't come this weekend. I've got to do some extra studying and stuff."

Kevin gave me a weird look. "You? Extra studying?" Kevin knew I was racking up an A average without breaking a sweat. He looked surprised.

"Yeah," I said. "Sorry." Then I slunk away as quickly as I could.

Kevin kind of started leaving me alone after that, though I could tell he didn't know why I'd changed. A few weeks later, he gave it one more try. It was after school. I was just walking out of the building, when he came up behind me.

"Uh, Megan, hi," he began, stuffing his hands in his pockets.

He looked as uncomfortable as I felt. I quickly looked to see if Rosemary or any of her friends were around. Fortunately, they weren't.

"Hi, Kevin," I mumbled, still walking ahead of him.

"Wait a minute, will you?" he said.

"I'm kind of in a hurry," I lied.

"Well, um," he stammered, as he came up beside me. "I was just wondering if you knew about the chess exhibition. It's downtown on Sunday. Hector Cabrini—the grandmaster?— is going to play sixteen matches blindfolded. My parents are driving me, and I was wondering, um, if—"

I cut him off. "Oh, I can't, Kevin. I have to study. I have a big French test next week."

What a lame excuse! I really did have a French test coming up, but Kevin and I both knew I didn't have to chain myself to my desk to study for it.

"Oh," he said, sighing. "Well, I wasn't asking you, actually." I could tell he was dying of embarrassment. "I was just wondering if you saw the article about it in the newspaper. It was kind of interesting."

"Oh. No, I didn't," I said, biting my lip and staring straight ahead.

"Okay. See you tomorrow," he said, shuffling off in the other direction. I felt like a real jerk. I should have gone after him, but I didn't.

Rosemary called me up that night. After I'd told her the answers to the biology homework, she asked, "So what are you going to wear tomorrow?"

It wasn't the first time she'd asked that. She and her friends always planned their outfits and talked about them with each other.

"Oh, I don't know," I answered, twisting the phone cord around my hand. "Probably just jeans."

"You never wear that pink sweater," she said. "The one with the shells."

The sweater was still in the shopping bag. "I know," I confessed. "It's kind of itchy."

"But it looks fabulous," she said firmly. "And I was thinking. You know your party dress? The skirt would go great with that sweater."

"Pink and red? I don't know," I said.

"Well, I do. I just read a whole article about wearing stuff that doesn't match. It's a whole new trend."

I didn't know what to say, so I didn't say anything.

"I think you should wear it tomorrow," Roe told me.

Well, that's just what I did. The weather was warming up a little, so I slipped on the mini-skirt and pulled the pink sweater over it.

My mother gave me a strange look when I came down to breakfast. "I'm not going to say a word," she said, reaching for her coffee cup.

I gulped down some cereal and took off for school. When I got there, I saw Roe inside the main entrance.

"Did you wear it?" she asked.

I nodded my head and took off my coat.

"Cool!" she cooed. "But isn't the sweater supposed to be off the shoulder?"

"I guess so," I said.

She pulled me into the girls' room. "Now, let me fix this," she said, tugging at the sweater so that it exposed my shoulder. "And you could use some extra make-up." She started brushing pink powder on my eyelids and cheeks.

"Now you look really radical," she told me when she was finished. "You know, Megan, you really should think about getting a boy-friend."

I looked in the mirror. My reddish brown curls were teased in the back, and my hazel eyes were surrounded by pink powder.

"I don't know," I murmured.

"You don't know?" Roe said with a laugh. "Well, I do. And you look fabu!"

I felt like people were staring at me all morning. It didn't help that my sweater jangled with every step I took.

At lunch, Roe and her friends were gushing all over me, telling me how great I looked. But I couldn't help noticing the confused stares of the other students.

I almost died when Vance Lockwood, the boy from the party, stopped by our table.

"Cute sweater," he said, staring at my bare shoulder. "I like the style." He gave me a weird wink and sauntered off.

"Ooh, Megan," Farrah cooed. "Someone likes you!"

"I told her she should dress differently," Rosemary told Farrah.

"Listen, guys," I said, "I'll see you later."

"Where are you going?" Heather asked.

"Oh, just to take a walk," I lied. The truth was, I had to hide. More than anything, I wanted to be alone.

"Okay. But I'll call you later," Rosemary said. We both knew what that meant. She needed the answers to the biology assignment.

I emptied my tray and hurried out of the cafeteria. I didn't stop till I was safely in the girls' room, locked in one of the stalls. I planned on staying there as long as I could, so I wouldn't have to face any more stares.

Finally, the bell rang. I was about to go get my books and head for my next class, when a group of girls burst into the bathroom. They were giggling loudly.

It was Rosemary and the others. I started to open the stall door to say hi, but something stopped me. I stood there with my hand on the lock, but I didn't turn it.

"Couldn't you die?" Rosemary squealed between guffaws. "Couldn't you just totally expire?"

They were screaming with laughter. I wanted to come out and join in. I mean, whatever they were talking about sure sounded hysterical.

"She is the most ridiculous person I've ever seen!" Heather chimed in. "How can she not know?"

"Obviously, she doesn't," Farrah purred. "She's totally oblivious."

"How do you keep it up, Rosemary?" Heather asked. "I could never keep a straight face."

"Hey," Rosemary said, "when I get my A in biology, it will all have been worth it. Every painful, boring moment."

The bottom dropped right out of my stomach. Suddenly, I couldn't breathe, let alone move.

"That sweater!" Heather moaned. "Ugh! I can't believe we talked her into buying it."

Rosemary laughed. "She'll buy anything I tell her to. She's desperate for me to like her. Just like a little doggy."

"Yup," Heather agreed. "Woof! Woof!"

"Here, Megan! Come, girl!" Rosemary said as if she were talking to a dog. Then she burst out giggling. I just stood there, a horrible feeling making its way up my insides.

They were talking about *me*!

CHAPTER

In that horrifying second, it all finally made sense. Those giggles on my first day of school . . . the stupid clothes they made me buy . . . the way they encouraged me to slather on make-up.

They'd been leading me on the whole time. All I had really ever been to Rosemary Weil was a brain for rent—and a good laugh.

I couldn't stand it another second. I burst out of that stall like a cannonball, screaming at the top of my lungs. "I HEARD EVERY WORD! I HEARD EVERYTHING! EVERYTHING!"

I barely kept my fists to myself. They stayed pinned to my sides, although I wish I had let them fly. Rosemary certainly deserved it.

After an initial look of pure shock, Rosemary gave me a cool stare. "So what if you heard?" she said in a breezy voice. "You're *still* going to help me on the biology test."

I was speechless. How could that girl think that I'd help her do *anything*?

In a moment, she explained. "Because if you don't, you'll be finished at Midway. No one will ever speak to you again."

"Big deal! Who cares if a bunch of phonies don't speak to me?" I stormed out of the girls' room with tears stinging my eyes.

All weekend, I holed up in my room and studied for the biology test. I didn't want to risk getting anything less than an A-plus on it.

On Monday, when Rosemary walked into biology, I just glared at her. Ms. Cornwall passed out our papers, and I answered all the questions with one hand cupped around the test so no one could see my answers.

Rosemary looked terrified. And though I'm not proud of it, I've got to say that I enjoyed the sight of her crashing in flames. That moment was sweet.

But it was the only sweet moment I had for the next few weeks.

The following morning in homeroom, I walked over to Kevin. "Hi," I said.

He just nodded. Then he opened a book and

pretended to be studying. I knew that trick well enough. Feeling about two inches tall, I waited for the bell to ring.

All that morning, the girls who had been so friendly to me before iced me out. When I walked down the hall, they seemed to slide out of my way.

At lunch, I had to pass by Jason Wright after I got my food. He was talking to Vance. "What do you get when you cross a clown with a dog?" Jason asked loudly.

"Don't tell me. I already know," Vance answered. "Megan Murray!"

They didn't even have the decency to stop laughing when I walked by. In fact, they laughed even louder. My head was spinning from the humiliation. It was all I could do to get to a free seat.

It so happened that the free seat was next to Stacy Bruller. She was a friend of Rosemary's, but not a very close one.

"Hi, Stacy," I said, giving her my best smile.

Without a word or a look, Stacy stood up and moved to another table.

From behind me, I heard someone else say, "Don't sit there. That's the nerd table." I whipped my head around, but I couldn't tell who'd said it. A whole bunch of kids were looking at me and laughing.

On the other end of the cafeteria, I saw Terri

leaving. Part of me wanted to run up to her and tell her I was sorry for the way I'd treated her. But it was too late. She was already gone.

I sat at that table, all by myself, not even picking at my lunch. I had certainly had my ups and downs since coming to Midway, but this was the absolute pits.

And who was really to blame? Biting my lip and holding back tears, I tried to tell myself it was all Rosemary Weil's fault. Or Heather's. Or Farrah's. But I couldn't escape the truth.

There were only three people responsible for the mess my life had become. And those three were me, myself, and I.

I'd let Amanda slip away, just because she lived in another town. I could have called her more often and kept in touch, but I'd been too lazy. I could have found a way to go visit her, too, if I had really tried.

I'd rejected Terri and Kevin, just because Rosemary didn't like them. Was it any wonder those two had finally given up on me?

The week went by, but it felt like years. Then Friday night, at my absolute low point, I had a dream—a very weird dream.

I was staring into the mirror, and my reflection was talking to me. I mean *I* wasn't talking, but *it* was.

"Rosemary," it was saying, "Rosemary, you've changed . . ."

"I'm not Rosemary!" I said. "I'm nothing like her!"

My reflection laughed at me. Then it slowly turned into a horror mask of Rosemary's face.

I screamed.

"Quiet!" the Rosemary mask said. "Shut up!" Suddenly, two clawlike hands reached out of the mirror, grabbed my arms, and started shaking me. I screamed and screamed . . .

"Megan!" my mother was shouting at me, holding me by the arms. "Honey, wake up! You're having a nightmare."

I couldn't get back to sleep, so I lay there thinking about the mess I was in. It was painfully clear to me what an idiot I'd been. From my very first moment at Midway, I'd tried to hide who I really was, so that people wouldn't reject me.

Well, that was all over, I decided. I actually began to feel happy. I got out of bed and went to the mirror. The evil mask of Rosemary Weil was gone. There was only me there—Megan Murray—and for once, I *liked* the face I saw.

"Amanda? It's me. Megan."

There was silence on the other end of the line. Then she said, "Megan! I can't believe it—it's so great to hear your voice!"

"I'm so sorry, Amanda, I've been such a

dweeb. I meant to call you a hundred times, but—"

"Don't be ridiculous," she said. "You were busy, and you forgot. It happens, Megan."

"Not to us. It shouldn't have happened. But I was too busy running after my new friends, and I was so embarrassed about not calling you for so long, that I—"

"Megan, will you stop? I forgive you. We're still best friends, at least as far as I'm concerned."

She meant it. I could tell. I started sobbing. Soon I was crying bucketfuls as I told her the whole horrible story.

"Oh, Megan," she said when I had finished. "I'm so, so sorry. How can I help?"

"You already have," I told her. "Just talking to you helps. Just knowing I have a real friend." I started sobbing again, but then I remembered what I had called to ask her. "But I do need to ask your advice," I said. "I've got to make it up to Kevin. I've got to show him I'm sorry. Oh Amanda, he's just got to forgive me!"

"Hmmm," she said, and I could almost hear her brain ticking. "Maybe a gift? Is there anything you could do for him, or buy for him?"

"He's not the kind you get flowers or candy for," I said, trying to think of something.

"Wait a minute," Amanda broke in. "Didn't you tell me he was into shortwave radio?"

"Yes."

"Wasn't there some antenna or something you said he wanted?"

"Of course!" I said, jumping off the bed in my excitement. Then I sank back down. "It's no good. That antenna costs over a hundred dollars, and I'm flat broke. I bought all these horrible clothes with Rosemary." I looked over at them hanging in the closet. At that moment I felt like ripping them to shreds.

"Couldn't you return them?" she suggested.

I thought feverishly. "I never wore the slacks, and I only wore the sweater once. But it's been three weeks, and the limit on returns is ten days."

"Try," Amanda said. Ordered, really. She is the greatest, she really is. "Make them take it back, Megan. You can do it."

I knew she was right. I had to do it, and I was going to do it, no matter what. "Still," I said, "that leaves me short by a lot. I could do some baby-sitting, I guess."

"I'll lend you the rest, Megan," Amanda said. "I know you're good for it."

"Amanda, I couldn't—"

"Yes you can. I want to help. It'll make me feel good, okay?"

I laughed. "It's a deal," I said. "Now, I'm going straight over and return these clothes!"

As soon as I hung up, I put the clothes in a bag with the receipt and raced downstairs.

"Mom," I said, hurrying into the kitchen. "Can you take me to the mall right away?"

My mother looked up from the potatoes she was peeling. "What for?"

"I have to return some things."

"How can you do that, Megan? Didn't you try them on when you bought them?"

I could have lied, and I almost did. But fortunately, I caught myself. "Yes, and they fit," I told her. "But they're horrible. And I look stupid in them."

"That's no reason to—"

"Mom, I'm not a little kid anymore," I interrupted her. "Please let me handle this the way I think is best."

She gave me a look, as if she was impressed. Then, she put down her paring knife. "Come on," she said. "Let's go."

I could have kissed her. Tomorrow, I promised myself, I'd vacuum the whole house.

"Do you want me to come in with you?" my mom asked as we pulled into the mall parking lot.

"No, thanks, Mom," I said. "This is something I've got to do for myself."

She gave me a kiss. "Good luck, Megan,"

she said. "I'll be at Shoe-O-Rama if you want me."

I ran up to Shazam. "I have a return," I told the woman behind the counter.

"Do you have a receipt?" she asked, looking at me over the top of her glasses.

I handed her the paper and bit my lip.

"I'm sorry," she said, shaking her head. "These were purchased over two weeks ago. I can't possibly refund your money."

"May I see the manager?" I asked, my voice trembling. I just couldn't take no for an answer.

"You can go into Mr. Fein's office, but I'm sure he won't—"

I scooted around the counter and into the office she was pointing to. Mr. Fein was working at a desk. He lifted up his bald head and gave me a startled look.

"Mr. Fein," I began. "I know about your store policy, but you've got to refund my money for these two items. The slacks still have the tags on them, and I only wore the sweater once."

"Is there a problem with them?" he asked, trying to be nice.

"No—I mean, yes. That is—I need the money! Do you want to hear the whole story?" I was actually willing to tell him everything, accompanied by real tears.

Thankfully, he didn't want to hear it. "Look, I really can't do this for you," he said. "If I do, I have to do it for everyone."

"No you don't!" I pleaded. "I promise I won't tell a soul. Honest!"

"You're broadcasting it to everyone in the store right now," he said under his breath. I could tell he was starting to get annoyed.

"Sorry," I mumbled, staring back out through the open door of his office. Turning back to him, my eyes focused on a picture of three little kids on his desk. "Are those your children?"

"Why yes, they are," he said, cracking a proud smile.

"Well, aren't you in luck!" I said. "I happen to be the world's best baby sitter. If you let me return these clothes, I'm willing to make you a special offer—I'll baby-sit for you ten times, absolutely free!"

That got him. I had the strange feeling his little "angels" had horns on top of their heads. I didn't care, though. I was going to get Kevin that antenna, no matter what.

He looked me up and down, thinking it over. "It's a deal," he said, grabbing the sweater from me. "Come with me to the register, quickly. And don't you dare tell a soul that I took a return after three weeks."

"You have my word of honor, sir," I said, holding my hand over my heart.

"Be at this address, Sunday at six," he said, scribbling it down and handing me the piece of paper—and my money.

I ran for Shoe-O-Rama, whooping for joy. I had done it! That antenna was as good as in my hands.

Now—how to get it into *Kevin's*?

CHAPTER

12

The next day, I visited Amanda and borrowed thirty dollars from her. Then I bought the antenna and gift-wrapped it. I added an "I'm sorry" card. That part was Amanda's idea.

My big problem was how to give the present to Kevin when he wasn't even speaking to me. I didn't want to bring it to school and give it to him in front of everybody.

As for dropping it at his door, ringing the bell, and running—well, I considered it briefly. But that was the coward's way out. I wasn't about to be a coward again. Not ever.

What I had to do was get together with him, and put it in his hands. I figured, even if I died of embarrassment at least it would be over quickly.

"When are we seeing the MacArthurs?" I asked my mom that night.

"We didn't have any plans," she said. "Why?"

"Oh, I was just wondering." I still hadn't told her why I'd bought the antenna, although she'd gone to the store with me, and I'd told her it was for Kevin. And she knew it wasn't his birthday. But I didn't explain and she didn't pry. I guess I have to give her credit. She had really gotten better about that sort of thing, I noticed.

"Oh, Megan," she said, a few days later, "I made plans with the MacArthurs for dinner on Friday night."

At school that Friday, I could see the discomfort on Kevin's face. I knew his parents had told him we were coming over. When I walked into his house that night, he looked positively green.

"Hi, Kevin," I said, smiling my nicest smile.

He said "Hi," to the floor and turned on his heels, heading into the kitchen to get away.

"Kevin," his mother called. "Dinner's not ready yet. Why don't you and Megan go up to your room and play?"

"Mo-omm!" Kevin groaned. "We're not babies anymore."

"Oh, I forgot," his mom said. "Don't teenagers play?"

"Come on, Kevin," I said, stepping in to save him any further embarrassment. He followed me upstairs.

The antenna had come unassembled, in a small box. I had the gift-wrapped box under my jacket so Kevin wouldn't see it. I didn't really have to bother hiding it, though. Kevin was looking at the floor the whole time anyway.

The minute we got to his room, I said, "Kevin, I'm sorry I've been such a jerk." Then, before he could answer, I stuck the package in his hands and said, "For you. For being so nice."

He looked stunned, I'll tell you. And when he opened it and saw what was inside—well, I've never seen a more surprised look on a person's face. "What?" he said. "I—I can't believe this! What did you—? Megan! My antenna! But how—?"

"Never mind," I told him. "It's a present. From me to you."

"But Megan, it must have cost you—"

"Come on, let's go try it out."

So we did. It only took us five minutes to assemble. We got the Virgin Islands first thing. Then there was a guy speaking Spanish, who sounded very far away, but we had to go eat dinner, so we never found out where he was from.

Before we went downstairs to eat, Kevin reached out and gave me a big hug. "Oh, Megan," he said in my ear. "You're—you're incredible. I can't believe you did this for me."

"Does that mean you forgive me for being such an idiot?" I asked.

"Come on, you weren't being an idiot."

"Oh, yes I was. You don't have to argue with me."

He looked me right in the eye. He was grinning. "Okay, I won't argue. But at least let me make it up to you a little. What can I get you?"

"Hmmm," I said. "Okay. How about a fruit smoothie at the mall tomorrow? Your treat."

"Forget it, Megan, that's nothing compared with—"

"It's what I want," I insisted. It was more than I deserved, considering the way I had treated him.

He let out a sigh, but I could see his face light up. "Then it's what you get," he said, taking my hand and leading me downstairs.

I could not have afforded a fruit smoothie on my own. Not even part of one. I was flat broke, in debt, even. But did I care? Not one bit.

We didn't say much as we sat there, sipping our fruit smoothies. But something was coming over me inside. It was a rush of feeling, kind of like waves—good waves, but overwhelming. I looked over at Kevin. He was sort of staring into space, and I wondered if he was feeling weird, too.

Maybe the fruit smoothies have gone bad, I thought. But no, they tasted fine. It was being here, with Kevin, here at the mall where Rosemary or anyone could see us.

Suddenly I realized that Kevin was really kind of good-looking. It wasn't just his new glasses, either, or that he was taller. It was his eyes. They were full of intelligence, and funniness, and feelings.

Then it hit me. Could this actually be what falling in love is? I pushed the thought to the back of my mind immediately.

Kevin glanced at me, and I held my breath. "Um, Megan? Did, uh . . ." He trailed off and looked down at the table.

Then he lifted his head again, a determined look in his eyes. Slowly, he leaned over the table.

My heart was beating a thousand times a minute as I gazed into his eyes.

I put down my spoon and leaned over the table. My eyes closed as I waited for his lips to touch mine.

I felt them, like a feather, soft and gentle. It was the most sensational experience!

When I leaned back again and opened my eyes, I was tingling from head to toenail.

"Wow," he said. It came out more like a squeak.

"Wow," I agreed. My voice sounded a little strange, too. My heart was pounding so hard it was pushing into my throat.

"We should do that again sometime," he said, and let out a little laugh.

"Yeah, we should," I said, nodding.

"Right." We both laughed. Something big was going on, and we both needed time to digest it.

"Hey, you guys!" came a familiar voice from behind me. I turned around. It was Terri Lawson, in her cheerleading captain's uniform. "Megan, I haven't seen you in a long time. How's it going?"

I was floored. Here she was, still being friendly to me after all this time, after the way I'd rejected her. She hadn't held it against me at all!

I could see now what a really sweet person Terri was. I mean, I always sort of guessed it, but let me tell you, it's how people act when it counts that matters.

"Great!" I said, clearly hearing the happiness in my own voice.

"Yeah, you seem good," Terri said. "I heard Rosemary's bunch making cracks about you, so I figured something must have happened."

"Something did," I said.

"Well," she said, breaking into a big smile, "you don't seem too upset about it."

"I'm glad it happened," I said proudly. It was true, too.

"I couldn't really see you and Rosemary or Farrah as friends," Terri said. "But I didn't want to say anything."

I understood. "Want to sit down and join us?" I said.

"Oh, I'd like to, but I've got to get to the game. Basketball playoffs, you know."

"Right," I said, as if I knew all about it. "Well, good luck. I hope we win."

"Hey, listen, maybe you'd like to come to the party tonight," she suddenly said. "Win or lose, we're getting together at my house. I know it's last minute, but if you're free—?"

I was free, all right. "Sure!" I said.

"Um, it's a boy-girl party. But lots of kids will be there without dates. If you want to bring somebody, though—" She glanced at Kevin.

I looked at Kevin, too. He nodded at me, taking my hand.

"We'll be there," I told Terri, flashing the grin that ate Pittsburgh.

"Great!" Terri said. "See you then. I live at 120 Windemere Terrace. The party starts about seven o'clock." With that, she ran off, waving.

She hadn't been gone thirty seconds when who should troop by but Rosemary and her gang. When they saw Kevin and me holding hands, you should have heard the giggles. They echoed back and forth across the Food Court.

But I didn't care. I held onto Kevin's hand and looked into his eyes. I didn't care a bit about giggles, insults, and petty remarks.

I had Kevin, I had Terri—hey, I even had Amanda! My parents were the best on earth, and I was the luckiest girl in the world. So maybe life wasn't so bad after all. In fact, it just might be perfect!